A SMOKY MOUNTAIN odyssey

May you have peace

Bill Pealey

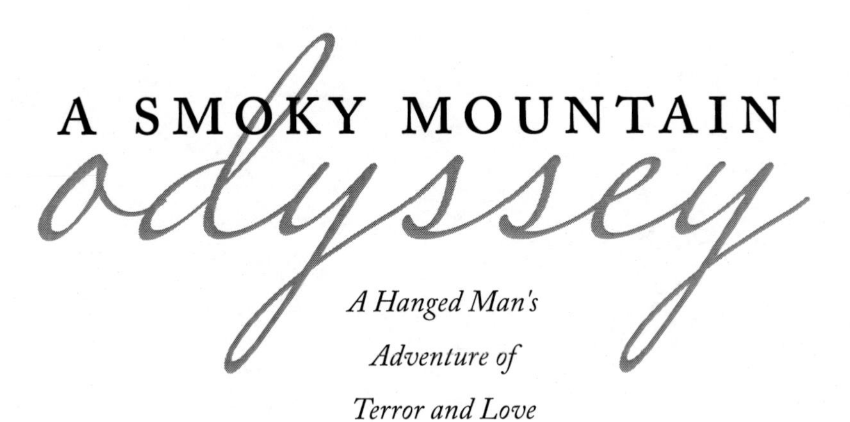
A SMOKY MOUNTAIN odyssey

A Hanged Man's Adventure of Terror and Love

BILL PENLEY

TATE PUBLISHING AND ENTERPRISES, LLC

Published by Tate Publishing & Enterprises, LLC
127 E. Trade Center Terrace | Mustang, Oklahoma 73064 USA
1.888.361.9473 | www.tatepublishing.com

Tate Publishing is committed to excellence in the publishing industry. The company reflects the philosophy established by the founders, based on Psalm 68:11,
"The Lord gave the word and great was the company of those who published it."

Cover design by Allen Jomoc
Interior design by Caypeeline Casas

Published in the United States of America

ISBN: 978-1-62295-634-0
1. Fiction / Action & Adventure
2. Fiction / Historical
13.04.03

CHAPTER 1

Sky Boys sat alone, in a lonely place. From there he surveyed the valley floor, two thousand feet below. Above him, he saw the crest of the Eastern Continental Divide, another two thousand feet. He had stopped, resting his mules that labored hard pulling a laden wagon up a crude road. Sitting on his wagon seat, he looked back down and counted six switchbacks where the road zigzagged up the mountain, decreasing the steep grade.

His vision froze. Something moved far below. It was only a speck. He focused his field glasses on a lone rider moving up the road. Sky mused, *Who might this man be?* Only people with purpose traversed these roads into wild country. The Smokies were drowsing at this hour, preparing to lower her shades for night.

He pondered the mysterious person while he scotched his wagon and unhitched his rig. Then he fed and watered his animals. After first tending to their needs, he set up camp, struck a fire, filled his coffeepot, and prepared a lean mountain supper. As he ate, birds serenaded him. They sang to gather themselves for day's end. Crows argued over their roosting places. An owl hooted. His mate sent her secret reply.

He filled his cup, and his tired muscles began relaxing. His five-and-one-half-foot frame sat leaning against an ancient stump. His hair, a robin's breast red, blended in with old moss that pillowed his head.

Sky's lonesomeness drew Willa, his sweetheart, into his thoughts. He could smell her auburn hair and see her blue eyes dancing at the sound of his voice. Her touch produced the sensation of warm honey on his skin. Closing his eyes, he envisioned her petite and trim body. Her afterimage enlivened the love that dared not speak its name.

His reverie ended when his mules brayed and pointed their ears toward a lone rider.

Now there's a dandy, if I ever saw one. Sky chuckled to himself. The man sat stiff in the saddle. He hugged the fenders between his legs and gripped the saddle horn with both hands.

A city slicker for sure. Although covered with trail dust, the man's pants, jacket, vest, and hat looked new and matched in color. His awkward body bounced on the saddle. His eyes and ears appeared small on his round face. Sky stood, smiling. "Stranger, howdy." He adjusted his cap. "Welcome to my campfire. I've a pot simmering. It may taste like barbed wire extract, but it's coffee. I've jerky and cornpone I'll share. I'm Sky Boys from over in Best, near Asheville."

The stranger said nothing, possibly caught off guard by Sky's friendliness. He looked left and right, studying the surroundings.

"Hop down off that fancy hoss and let him rest," Sky continued. "That's a hard pull back there."

The man threw his left leg over his saddle to swing down. *The dude needs lessons on mounting a horse and getting off*, Sky concluded. The well-trained roan shied from the man's wrong-side dismount.

The stranger offered a weak, limber-wrist handshake, and then blinked twice. "Uh…I'm from… uh… Kentucky."

"Looks like you need to walk and limber your joints. Lead that fine hoss over there to the branch for a long drink. Swallow some down for yourself. It'll cool your innards."

He studied the man. "Where'd you travel from today? I left Old Fort this morning, pulling goods up for our mountain folks. I don't recollect seeing you before."

"In fact, young man, I'm just passing through." The man measured his words, obviously thrown off balance by Sky's questions and openness.

"It won't be long before the sun yonder will be behind ole Smoky." Sky shaded his eyes for a quick look at the horizon. "How 'bout stripping that fine animal and give him a rubdown. He needs it after climbing that mountain. You might as well fetch your bedroll and sleep here for the night. The next bed-down spot will be a mile or more up the road, and dark is almost here."

He spit in his palms and picked up his ax. "I'll chop some extra firewood so we can set up and talk a spell." He took his stone and touched the ax blade. "My paw told me, 'A minute spent sharpening the ax saves an hour cutting.'"

The man gave no response and continued his clumsy efforts to unsaddle his horse. He tangled and untangled the bit and girth. The simple effort to unbridle the horse's head gave Sky a chuckle. Finally, he tied the lead rope to a tree.

"Obliged," the man answered. "I guess I did run a bit low on my travel needs today."

Sky fed the roan grain for the night. He hugged his neck and patted his rump. "Mister, that's the finest hoss I've ever seen. Where'd you get such an animal? He looks like an Arabian to me." The man didn't reply.

His work finished, Sky sat with crossed legs beside the fire and rolled a smoke. He pretended total concentration on his tobacco but watched askance every move of the man, who seemed to come from nowhere. After tossing aside his coat and hat, he brought a new-looking blanket, along with a jug of liquor with his saddle bag to the campfire. Groaning, he folded his stiff legs and sat. He loosened his belt to relieve the pressure on his ample belly.

Sky fetched a burning twig from the fire and, while lighting his cigarette, heard a gulp. He turned and saw the man downing a long swig of whiskey, blinking hard to recover from the alcohol burn in his throat. Face red from the sudden flush of liquor, he passed the jug to Sky. "Here, fellow, have a drink on me. Name's Brisco."

The hooch appeared to embolden Brisco and loosen his tongue. He slid a deck of cards from his pocket. Now, smiling, he proposed, "What do you say we play a game of poker, Sky? Do you have any money on you?"

Sky's sensibilities ignited. He'd spent hundreds of hours with his uncle Sunday, who had been a professional gambler in his past. Loving the game, Sky had honed his poker skills, using shelled corn for money. Uncle Sunday had perfected in him the knowledge and memory of cards and how to interpret the body language of opponents. He learned how to spot and counter a cheat.

"Shucks, I've only got a mite of change. I just haul stuff down the mountain to Lowlanders and bring trade goods back up to the mountain settlers. They mostly barter for their needs. Cash is scarce in these mountains. Many folks have never seen any real money."

He let that explanation soak in while he studied every expression, gesture, and squint made by the man he suspected was up to no good. He clinked his change and volunteered, "I don't know much about cards, but if you'll teach me as we go along, I'll give 'er a shot, and what little coins I've saved, I'll bet. Maybe I'll get lucky and add some more."

Brisco slipped a faint smile and licked his lips. "Now here's how it's done." He spoke as if to a child. "We put our money on the ground and play for the highest number in pairs." He gave a lesson about kings, queens, jacks, and building pairs and straights. "Think you know enough to get started, eh, friend?" He rolled his shirt sleeves, stretched his arms, and limbered his fingers.

Sky studied him like a cat watching a mouse hole. Brisco riffled the cards and dealt. *Well, Uncle Sunday, here we go.* The mountain around them hushed, holding her breath. The campfire cast spooky shadows. The horse whinnied. A mule pawed.

Sky won first with a decent hand. Brisco congratulated him loudly. "See there, you're a lucky man."

Over and over Sky questioned Brisco, pretending inexperience. Brisco's confidence mounted. When darkness fell, Sky lit a lantern, and the game turned serious. Sky's change became folding money, and Brisco began to show panic. His hands trembled, and his breathing quickened. His jug became lighter as Sky's pot grew heavier. Brisco yanked a wad of bills from his pocket. Sky pretended hesitancy. "I donno 'bout this, Brisco. I've never seen folding stuff like that, but heck, I started with pert-near nothing, losing it is the worst I can do." His winnings accumulated.

Brisco's booze ran low from his frequent guzzles. In a flash, his demeanor turned to anger. "You've wiped me out. It's not fair, you winning, not knowing how to play." He threw his empty jug aside and staggered to his saddlebags. He brought back a leather pouch, out of which he poured ten twenty-dollar gold coins.

Sky's eyes popped. "Are you sure you want to gamble that?"

"You mighty right, mule-skinner." Brisco's words slurred, now that the firewater had taken effect.

"I've never seen any gold money. Maybe we ought to quit now." Sky stood. "I've made more money than I've ever had. Why don't you hold on to your gold?"

"Don't you renege on me, you hick backwoodsman." He slammed a gold piece to the ground. "Sit back down and cover that, you stupid galoot. I'll teach you what real card playing is. Now cover it and deal."

Sky's nerves were on razor edge. Lessons taught by Uncle Sunday fired in his recollection. Then as if sent by a muse, Uncle Sunday whispered, "Relax, stay calm, and don't let your opponent read your emotions or bluffs." He relaxed, took a deep breath, and began to study Brisco carefully, every tick, wink, twinkle, tap, and nod. Never had he felt the tension of that moment.

They shuffled. They cut and drew. They pondered. They bet and rose. They called. Witnessing the game at stake, the universe paused—or so it seemed.

Brisco dealt, upped the ante, and won the pot, building his drunken high spirits. Sky slowed things down. He questioned a simple point, faking ignorance, and lost again. Overconfident, Brisco became careless. Sky possessed the ten gold coins in less than an hour.

Brisco yanked a gold watch from his pocket and demanded Sky to match it with two gold pieces. "We'll cut the deck and draw, high card win. That'll change your cussed luck."

Sky drew a five of hearts. Brisco lost the watch with a three of clubs.

He sprang up, snatching a large stick of firewood. "You've cheated me. I'll send you to hell for it."

He swung at Sky's head. Dodging, Sky grabbed his ax to use the handle for protection. Brisco, staggering, lost his balance and fell head first into the ax blade, slicing his face and opening his skull. He fell like lightning had struck him, dead, before thumping to the ground. Blood, mingled with brains, flowed from the huge gash.

Sky's knees buckled when he saw the horrible scene. He struggled for composure, but the flowing of blood and stench from some of it that splashed into the fire threw him into a retching convulsion.

This cannot be real. I'm having a nightmare. I must awake. God help me. Only a deathlike silence answered him. *Lord, what must I do?*

Frenzied, he quickly fed and watered the mules and then hitched them to the wagon. He examined the tie-downs, wheels, and mule's gear.

He refused to look at Brisco's body. Now he faced the inevitable. *Load him on the wagon. Get him away from here, now. Decide what to do later.*

He leaned his muscular frame over Brisco, slipped his arm under the upper body, and lifted. As the air exhaled from the dead man's lungs, it created a growl from the vocal cords. Sky yelled and jumped away, as if a panther had leaped at him. He collected himself and crept back to Brisco's gory cadaver.

Although similar in size, when he attempted to lift the corpse, the limp body—with its dangling arms, legs, and head—doubled its live weight, making it impossible. He grasped Brisco's ankles and tugged him up a bank to a level where he could drive the wagon alongside. After spreading Brisco's blanket to shield his cargo from any blood, he positioned the wagon and rolled the body over onto it. Sky outstretched Brisco's arms and legs and then tied them with a rope to the wagon sides. He tucked the saddle blanket around the foul bundle. Sweat ran down his face. As he wiped it, he pondered, *Has all the evidence been removed?*

When he looked back toward the fire, he saw a large pool of blood where the body had fallen and, from there, a blood-stained trail to the wagon.

Evidence of a disturbance remained, so, ax in hand, he cut pine bushes and swept over the roughed-up places. He gathered leaves into the mule's feed buckets to sprinkle over the incriminating area.

Sky had laid the money, gold coins, and watch aside, wishing he had never seen the hated loot. He considered throwing them down the mountainside. Instead, he stuffed the filthy things into his pockets and mounted the wagon. He felt his sanity stretched to the limit.

He heaved a deep sigh, clicked the mules, and the heavy wagon inched forward. The horse whinnied. He had forgotten the roan. Stopping, he rushed water and grain to the slighted animal. He also gathered up the overlooked coat and hat Brisco had carelessly thrown aside and tucked them into the wagon. He made a loose fit of the saddle onto the roan and tied him behind the wagon, and they rolled away.

The dirt road was bad to this point, but the rest of the way to the top presented a slope, steep and hazardous. Around the spine of the ridges, boulders could not be removed by using crude tools and horsepower available when widening the original trail was undertaken. Passage demanded extreme caution.

Sky lifted a spiritual request. *God, I don't have time to talk to you right now, but I'm asking for your help. Guide my mules that are feeling their way along in the moonlight.*

The wagon thumped and bumped and tossed. Sky faced hair-raising tasks. The mules had to be kept moving. If they stopped, either they could never regain momentum or the loaded wagon would roll backward, dragging the payload, animals, and the teamster to a gruesome death.

"Go! Git! Pull, mules! Get up!" Sky strained his lungs bellowing at the straining beasts. He slapped them with the lines, often mercilessly cracking his whip over their backs. He kept a bucket of rocks beside him, from which, in the most treacherous times, he threw on their rumps. They dared not stop! A ravine yawned, far below, a thousand feet or more, straight down. Waterfalls and white water tumbled over giant boulders at the bottom. The most dangerous place in the road had been chiseled off a sheer bluff. Sky had tied a rope over his lap to keep himself from being slung off the seat. To his knowledge, no one had attempted that terrifying trip at night. Only by some fate of providence and a full moon had he completed it.

The sun was peeping over the eastern horizon when Sky turned his panting mules off the road to give them rest. He felt tuckered out and sweat-drenched. Drained of strength, he lay across the wagon seat and slept.

Horseflies buzzing and biting him like bee stings awakened him. When he slapped at them, he saw a horrifying sight. His clothes, hands, and arms had been caked with blood that the darkness had hidden. He sprang from his seat and ran to a stream. After stripping, he stepped into the frigid water. He washed. He scrubbed. Not having soap, he took sand from the stream bottom and ground it across his body, head to toe. *Is my body clean? Will the events of the past night ever erase from my memory?* Completing all he could do to his body, he began washing the dried blood from his clothes. Downstream, the pristine water flowed red with the blood of a man who had died attempting to take the life of another.

Sky remembered the animals. He rushed several buckets full of water to them, until each had its fill. Then he fed them grain.

He walked around his wagon to check the condition and security of his load. There was no Brisco. Terrified, he ran, retracing his tracks. He stayed on the inside of the road, not daring to be near the precipice. As he approached the curve around the granite ridge, he slowed and saw slight evidence that something heavy had broken loose when the wagon bounced violently over the boulder. A trace of blood revealed where Brisco went over the edge.

Sky crawled on his hands and knees to the outer edge of the road. It was a sheer drop-off to the river. Any retrieval would be impossible. *Oh God, will that body ever be found?* He could hear his heart beating in his ears. Momentarily, he pondered jumping off the cliff. *Just one leap and this nightmare will end.*

In that moment he remembered Willa's last words. "Be careful, Sky. Come back to me." *She's waiting for me. I cannot do this to the one I love.* With that thought, he returned to his wagon and headed home.

Questions began flushing out of his mind like coveys of quails. *How will I explain this trip to hell and back? Should I tell the sheriff? Should I keep quiet and hope nobody finds out? Maybe Uncle Sunday will have an answer.*

CHAPTER 2

Sunday Boys knew from the sweat on the back of the mules and lather around their collars that they had been pressed beyond normal use. He watched as Sky pulled up in front of the barn then leaped off the wagon and began stripping gear from his mules. He had always worked gently with his animals, never pressing them with undue exertion.

From the doorway, Sunday studied Sky's impulsiveness, leaving equipment strewn haphazardly, adjusting his cap, and hitching his britches. Nothing was ordinary about his deportment.

Sky watered and fed his mules and gave each a rubdown with his usual kind words and a pat on each rump. When he began his quick-footed gait toward the house, Sunday stepped to the porch, presenting his usual smile and warm welcome to his nephew, although, by affection, he loved him more than any natural-born son he could have ever had.

"Uncle Sunday, I've played hell."

"Hold on, lad. Look at me. I've been to that place several times. Whatever the problem, we can work it out." He laid an assuring hand on Sky's shoulder.

"Sit, son. Roll yourself one while I stoke my pipe." The thin cigarette paper spilled more Bull Durham than it saved as Sky's trembling fingers worked at the makings. After Sunday puffed to light his meerschaum, he reached over and tipped Sky's roll with flame from the same match.

"Tell me about your trip."

"A man is dead because of me." Sky spoke faintly, voice wavering. He blinked, and tears began coursing through the dust on his face.

Years of experience had seasoned Sunday with wisdom. He moved close enough to Sky that his aura could be sensed, but he remained silent, allowing Sky to wash his bruised soul with tears.

Sunday's pipe burned out, and he sat, waiting. Only birds singing broke the silence. The breeze stirred gently, carrying with it the scent of honeysuckle. A humming bird visited a porch flower.

One of his housekeepers caught Sunday's gesture and brought a pitcher of freshly drawn water from the well. The cool refreshment drew from Sky a deep sigh.

"Now, son, tell me your story."

"It ain't pleasant, Uncle Sunday. I've failed your teaching. I've failed God. I've failed myself."

"Life always has unpleasant episodes. We grow through times of failure. Our mistakes make us into the unique individuals we were born to become. Whatever has happened will finally work out for your good in the end. Now, let's examine your situation. We can unravel it, no matter the problem."

Sky, from the beginning, laid out the past two days' happenings. He explained about Brisco, the man from nowhere, the card game, Brisco's death, his covering the scene and his efforts to haul the body out during the night, and then losing the body off his wagon and over the mountain bluff.

"Any chance the body can be found and retrieved?"

"No way. It tumbled off the wagon into the gorge where the crag fell sheer down on each side of the river. The laurel hells and ivy slicks above and below the falls would make it impossible to get to that spot even if someone knew it was down there."

"We must make careful preparation for the worst conditions," Sunday said. "Tomorrow we'll go into Asheville and confer with an attorney. We'll get a jump on whatever might turn up. Now, let's enjoy supper and get a good night's sleep.

"We've work to do tomorrow," he added. "Have faith, my boy. However it turns out will make you stronger in the future."

Sky had slept fitfully, even after a submissive prayer. The smell of country ham, biscuits, grits, and gravy drew him to a mountain breakfast, and he ate ravenously.

Sunday's horse and buggy were waiting, and the two began their three-hour journey from the village of Best to Asheville on the North Carolina turnpike.

The heavily traveled road had deep muddy ruts, wagon-wheel width. There was group after group of herdsmen driving flocks of turkeys, herds of cattle, horses, goats, and pigs being shifted from Tennessee to South Carolina, some going south, some north to the barter markets. Mingled in the muck was the stench of animal manure and urine. Because many of the drovers stayed overnight, there were rooms for rent and corrals behind the rooming houses to hold the stock. The amalgamation of smells never ceased. Flies buzzed. Mosquitoes chirred. Dogs barked continuously. Cursing among the herders was common. Their buggy wheeled by a roadside preacher warning sinners to repent.

Most of the houses along the turnpike were clustered around a water source, and most were constructed of logs, chinked with mud, and their roofs covered with rived wood shingles. Behind every dwelling stood an outhouse. Wet clothes hung to dry over tree limbs and bushes. Runny-nosed children sloshed through mud puddles, yelling and playing. The children and many adults were barefoot. Except for a few wealthier ones, poverty was the rule of life.

Sky sat somber, his thoughts confused; his dread deepened.

Sunday spoke as if his feelings had overflowed. "Sky, since you came to live with me, it has been immensely satisfying. You have worked hard, you have done well, and I'm proud of you. I never married. I have no children, but I consider you my son. In the evenings we visited and chatted, mostly we played cards. Regretfully, I have not shared my personal life and background with you because you have worked from sunup to sundown. Everyone has been consumed in putting their lives back together after the war that tore our nation asunder, especially our lives here in western North Carolina. Therefore, you and many others are not aware of the political struggle we here in these mountains are in."

"What are you driving at, Uncle? We're going to see someone about a dead man and explain how I didn't kill him. What has the war and politics got to do with me?"

"Regretfully everything, I'm afraid. Now that we have some time together, I'll give you a thumbnail sketch." The buggy bounced, dodged deeper holes, and wove in and out of herds and drivers. Sky noticed how Sunday paid no attention to vulgar shouts and some who sneered at his modern carriage and well-groomed clothes.

"Few mountain people, from the Piedmont west, can read. Most of them still have no clue why the Civil War was fought. The slavery issue meant little to them." Sunday frowned and pursed his lips. "They do, however, have a long generational memory. Most all of them had a great-great-great-granddaddy or other kin who were among the Over-Mountain-Men who marched down out of these mountains to Kings Mountain, in the Piedmont. Those backwoodsmen wore buckskins, homemade woolens, slouch hats, or beaver skin caps. They made their own gunpowder and carried their own provisions. Those sharp-eyed hunters, with no leader, had only their muzzle-loading rifles, a sharp knife, and a glint of determination in their eyes. The only thing those mountain warriors fought for was freedom—freedom to own their own land, freedom to make their own decisions and mistakes. Our mountain forebears were willing to die for that. When England was defeated in that Revolutionary War, our United States Constitution and Bill of Rights were established, and we became a nation."

He smiled as he glanced at Sky. "Those, our grandsires, bred and hammered into their children that our nation is one. Stand by her. No matter what comes, stand by your government."

As their buggy jolted along, Sky struggled to grab his uncle's words and tuck them into his memory. "I didn't know these things, Uncle Sunday, but how does that affect my problem?"

"I'm coming to that. Our southern states wanted to secede from the Union. Slavery was an issue, yes. But politics of one kind or another prevailed. Our western North Carolina people did not understand those matters. One thing they did know: support your government. Our freedom was bought with blood."

Sunday shifted his weight as they bounced through a pothole.

"Our mountaineers were divided, recruiters from the Northern and Southern armies came through these mountains. If a family did not yield men between the ages fifteen and thirty-five, they were killed, their houses burned, farm equipment confiscated, and livestock stolen. This was true of both the Union and Confederate armies.

"These things, and of course others, caused severe division. In some cases, brother fought against brother, cousin against cousin, and neighbor against neighbor."

"How about our family?"

"They were confused like most everybody else. The Boys family was leaning toward the Union, for the reasons I've told you. We didn't want our nation divided. However, there were some massive slaughters that took place around them by Union Bushwhackers." Sunday looked at Sky for emphasis. "It was in the heat of anger and revenge that your daddy joined the Confederate Army. None in the family faulted him. It cost him his life. That war split our nation and left wounds that will take years to heal."

The buggy pulled up at Attorney Anthony Chandler's office. When Sunday and Sky went inside, the two older men yelled jubilantly and embraced. After the wheels of friendship had been lubricated, Sunday came directly to the point.

"Tony, this is Sky, son of my brother Billy."

"Hello, Sky. I was saddened to learn of your father's death. He was a good man. Always be proud of him. You are from good stock."

"Thank you, sir."

Sky had never been in a lawyer's office. He looked in awe at the shelves lined with leather-bound books. Memorabilia from the Revolutionary War and even the recent Civil War were placed discretely around the room.

"Tony, Sky has become directly involved in an accident. He has told me the account. I'll let him explain the event to you. I want you to legally represent him. Spare no expense. You have carte blanche from me."

"Whatever is in my power and ability, I will execute. Now, Sky, from the beginning, tell me what happened."

Attorney Chandler stoked his pipe and listened paternally as Sky narrated his ordeal.

After listening and taking careful notes, the lawyer asked, "Are you certain no one else witnessed this incident?"

"As far as I know, there were none. I wish there had been. I did not intend to kill that man. I was trying to save my own life."

Attorney Chandler sat pensive. Time and again he relit his pipe. The smell of tobacco was strong. Smoke hung like haze in the room. Outside noise was muffled, but the silence inside was deafening. Sky sat fidgeting, rubbing his hands together, brushing fingers through his hair, drumming his fingertips. Sunday caught his eye and motioned silence.

At long last the lawyer broke the silence. "It is my opinion that we go and report this incident to the sheriff, now."

"Why must we do it now? That body may never turn up."

"That is true. However, since gold was discovered near Old Fort, prospectors are panning the beds of every branch, creek, and river for miles around. I suspect the body of that man you call Brisco will show up."

"I agree." Sunday nodded. "If the body is found, you will be in serious trouble, so let's make the first move."

Reluctantly, Sky consented. The trio walked to Sheriff Zachary Pearson's office.

The attorney spoke respectfully, "Good afternoon, Sheriff Pearson."

"Howdy, Tony. Have you done picked up some more Yankee scum to help out with their law breaking?"

Sunday saw a reaction from Sky and reached over, putting a soothing hand on his shoulder.

"As a matter of fact, Sheriff, this young man is the son of one of the Confederate fighting men. Actually, his father joined the Confederacy by his own initiative. He was not conscripted. Sheriff, this is Sky Boys, son of Billy Boys."

"On his own initiative, like hell! That whole bunch of Boys was all Union rabbles. I know what Billy done. He got mad when the Yankees cleaned out Shelton Laurel. That's what happened. He weren't no reb. Besides that, I know this here Sky Boys. He's the nit that tucked tail and run. He hid out when the Yanks wiped out that home of his'n. I never knowed he had come out of hidin'. What's he done now? Why you got him here?"

"Zack, the Civil War has been fought, and it's over. Everyone is trying to heal and put their lives back together. A majority of good people elected you to represent the law for them in a fair manner. I respect your sentiments. I honor your Confederate leaning, but Zack, we're all Americans now. We're no longer North and South. I respectfully ask you, in the name of democracy and in respect for the badge you wear, to let the past die and have a new beginning."

"Preacher, save your sermon for the church. How can I help you?"

"Sheriff Pearson, this is a grave affair. I will handle each detail to insure that justice is carried out. This matter may lead to a jury trial. Therefore, from this moment forward, I want all our facts exact, and I expect you to represent your office without prejudice. The time for vengeance has passed."

"Well, tarnation, Counselor, lay it out to me, and let's get on with it."

"This young man, Sky, has done well in his community. He has been honest, hard working, and honorable. He has begun a freighting business and prospered with it. I'm going to ask him to tell you the facts of an incident that took place a few hours ago."

Sky carefully detailed the tragedy. He emphasized how he had tied Brisco onto his wagon and was in the process of bringing his body in to turn over to the law when it bounced off and fell over the cliff.

"Sheriff, I have here the money, the gold coins, and the watch Sky won from the man in that poker game. I'm turning it over to you until the matter is finalized."

When Sky and Attorney Chandler had concluded, Sheriff Pearson immediately dismissed the three men and followed them out the door. "I'll get right on this. I'll head out for Old Fort today and see if we can't roust that body."

When the three men returned to Attorney Chandler's office, the wise attorney wanted to know, from the beginning, everything he could about Sky.

"Sunday, explain to me the matter which Zack mentioned regarding Sky hiding out. If not relevant to our case, it interests me."

"Let me work up to that by giving you an up-to-date rundown of myself over the past few years," Sunday suggested.

"As you know, I was not living here during the war. I left several years ago and went away to college. Afterward, I sailed to Europe and established a business to import merchandise for a clientele in the larger northeastern cities. When the War between the States broke out here in America, I remained abroad. Unmarried, with some money to lose, if necessary, I became a gambler playing among the elite between Paris and London. I've no intention to boast; however, I became considerably wealthy."

Anthony smiled and nodded his understanding.

"When the war clouds had settled, I came back to America and heard of the devastation, especially among my kin in these mountains. I invested my money securely and returned here. My family was gone, wiped out by enemies from both sides. I kept hearing about a nephew Sky."

Sky stretched out his ears. He reached and tucked into his memory stories that he had never heard.

"How did you find me, Uncle Sunday?"

"I located an old mountain man, for years a trusted friend of our family. He told me he might ask around and perhaps help me. When I recognized his impoverished condition, I gave him twenty dollars. Surprised with that gift, he immediately said, 'Let's go. I know whar that young un's at.'

"That old tobacco-spitting hill man almost walked me to death trying to keep up with his unbroken pace. We topped a ridge, and the old one gave an owl hoot. Soon, a reply came back. In ten minutes, we were in Sky's cave, which held his entire worldly possessions: a pot, skillet, an ax, a terrapin shell with hog lard and a wick for a dim light, a deer and bear skin, a hand mill to grind corn, parched acorns or chestnuts, and a thumb-creased family Bible. Without notice, the old one eased away and vanished into the forest."

"He did his job well," Chandler said.

Sunday nodded. "He did. It seems Sky, cunning and mountain-wise, had located the cave in a remote, south-facing mountainside, near a trickle of water, and he had stored away food for a hideout. When the Bushwhackers hit his family, he slipped away and survived in the wilderness."

Attorney Chandler was clearly enthralled by the odyssey and urged Sunday to continue.

"I took Sky into my home, and he has become a son to me. I established him in his freight business. Almost every night, for entertainment, we played poker, which he learned quite well. We played for hours at a time. My big mistake was failing to teach him how not to anger an opponent by wiping him out. I accept blame for him in this predicament today."

"None of that, Sunday. Even God cannot change the past. We take what life hands us and work with it." Chandler rose to his feet. "Come with me to my house. It's past noon, but the missus will have ample food. We'll come back here and discuss further legal matters."

Unlike many homes ravished by marauding armies, the Chandler house had been untouched, likely because of its unique seclusion. The furniture was new, imported in recent years from England, bearing the latest fashion of Victorian design. High ceilings suspended Venetian candle chandeliers. The walls displayed paintings in massive gilded frames, and plush carpets from the Orient insulated the floors.

Back at the office, after a sumptuous meal, small talk ended. Attorney Chandler laid out the circumstances as he foresaw them with earnest solemnity. "Sky, we must make plans for the worst scenario. I suspect that body will be recovered, and if it is, I am sure Sheriff Pearson will arrest and jail you."

"Please, sir, I don't understand. It was self-defense. Brisco was trying to kill me."

"I sympathize with your feelings, Sky. However, if that body turns up, I am certain we are in for a murder trial, based on circumstantial evidence. The trial will not be about Sky Boys. You will only be the scapegoat."

He shook his head. "We got a sample of the ignorance, prejudice, and hate that drives Sheriff Pearson. He is a rabid Confederate, in a lost cause. He wrongly uses his office to take vengeance on everyone who did not swear allegiance to the secessionist's cause. Your family was one of them. I stand proudly for the United States, but there are many lawyers and judges who are still seeking revenge. I work in the court system, and I have to tell you that local courts do not always hand down justice these days.

"Local magistrates can call whomever they choose to sit on juries, and some superior court judges tend to pick jurors from among local citizens who happen to share their personal convictions of right and wrong, disregarding all those abstract fine-print stipulations in the law books."

Sky sat with his mouth agape, unable to comprehend the facts he was hearing. "I have always obeyed the law. Ask anyone down where I live. They know I do."

The attorney countered, "Reputation, kinship, and even one's address have little to do with verdicts. Sadly, it is politics that often rule."

Sunday sat quietly, a frown furrowing his forehead.

"Sky, it is apparent you love your uncle. You have great pride in him and you should because he is a wise man. However, by many, especially the sheriff, he is hated, labeled a coward simply because he was away for the duration of the war. His prosperity is obvious, and many people are envious and jealous of him. I tell you these facts to help you understand what faces us.

"We are in the decade of post-war lawlessness. Our good government is in disarray. Our system of law is staggering. We are far from Raleigh, farther from Washington; thus, crime is rampant. Men, like Sheriff Pearson, will vent their hatred on you. These are hard words, Sky, but you must be prepared. I will give you my best representation."

Preparing for departure, Sunday gave the attorney a parcel of currency, reaffirming, "No money is to be spared in this case."

Sunday and Sky arrived home after dark, tired and weary.

"Let's eat and go to bed, Sky. Try to sleep. Trust the One who created you. He has cared for you until today, hasn't he?"

"Yes, Uncle, I'll trust as best I can."

Like every night, Sky's last thoughts were of Willa. Come morning, he awoke, still yearning for her. Friendship had conceived love, but their only expression had been sly touches and passionate gazes. During their last visit, he hugged her and whispered, "I love you." Recent events made him realize life was uncertain, and he must savor every moment.

He prepared a picnic and pointed his buggy toward Willa's home. After a courteous parental visit, he said, "Willa, let's ride out to the old Indian village site and have a picnic."

"Oh, I'd love that." Willa's blue eyes spoke as gaily as her merry voice. She had blossomed early and ripened fast. Now, at age twenty, she was a beautiful young woman with reddish-brown hair. He studied the graceful flow of her body as she scampered to the buggy. From the books Uncle Sunday had suggested he read, he concluded that the same designer who formed Iseult, Juliet, and Bathsheba had formed Willa. Her sounds, shifts, touches, and unique scent lingered in his memory. He discovered little personality wrinkles that make every woman different and wonderful.

The buggy rolled into the ancient clearing. "That weeping willow tree yonder"—Sky motioned—"was sacred to the Cherokees. The old timers say young lovers spent hours inside the ground sweeping boughs after their marriage intentions were announced."

"Can I see inside?"

"Of course. Let's go," he answered as he fetched the food basket. "It might be a good place to eat." As they parted the boughs and stepped inside, the ambience was Edenic.

They spread their food hurriedly and sat, their eyes riveted on each other. As if choreographed, Willa lifted a strawberry to Sky's mouth. "Taste this, my sweetheart." The touch of her lingering fingers on his lips was rapturous.

"Now one for you, my love." At his slightest touch, she threw her arms around him. Her body trembled as they melted together. He heard her gasp, followed by a deep sigh. She relaxed, satiated in his arms. He pondered her swollen lips, flushed cheeks, and glistening eyes. "Willa, I will always love you. There will never be another. Never!"

As if the heavens rose to applaud the drama, a thunderbolt jolted them back to reality. Storm clouds had gathered unexpectedly.

"We must hurry. Grab our belongings while I ready the horse and buggy." The rain came in a downpour. With no shelter, they pressed homeward in the topless carriage.

Without warning, a wheel rolled off its axle, throwing Willa off her seat onto the muddy ground, unconscious. Forgetting the rig, Sky leaped to kneel over her, shouting, "Willa, my love, come back to me!"

Her eyes blinked once, twice, and then she smiled. "I'm okay now. I have you. Let it rain. Let it pour!" She pulled him down over her body and let the sky, the mud, the storm, the universe witness their ecstatic passion.

The storm passed. "I'll replace the wheel. You step into the river and wash the mud off yourself. I'll join you shortly."

Willa always carried a petite pair of scissors in her purse. She cut a wee lock of her hair from the spot that carried the unique scent of fresh seashell and wrapped it in a square of cloth she cut from her dress hem. "Carry this"—she impishly grinned—"to remind you of this day."

Past sundown the two arrived back at Willa's home. "I'll explain our tardiness to your folks."

"They'll understand, Sky. They like you. Besides, I told them I will someday be your wife."

Four days later, Sheriff Zachary Pearson, along with two deputies, pulled up in front of Sunday Boys's house. The sheriff rode a horse; the deputies were atop a mule-drawn wagon.

"I've come in the name of the law," shouted the lawman, attracting all the attention he could to display his authority. "We found that feller with his head busted open. And we know Sky Boys done it. I'm a taking him in." He presented a warrant and with brute force took Sky into custody.

Willa stood among the crowd, weeping. During the past three days Sky had not hidden anything from her. She had vowed, "I won't ever love anybody but you, no matter what the future brings. I am yours forever!"

In spite of the outcry from the crowd, a deputy, under the sheriff's instructions, tied thongs around

Sky's wrists and secured him behind the wagon, making him walk to the pace of the mules. En route to the jail, he stumbled often and twice fell in the muddy road. People lined the turnpike; some shouted for, others against, the ignominy carried out before them.

When the posse reached the jailhouse pulling the prisoner, now drained of strength, the arrogant sheriff growled, "Cut the damned Yankee a loose and throw him in the slammer. I hope he rots in there and the rats eat on him. I can't wait to see this traitor hung."

Sky sat in a six-by-eight-feet cell, dank, dark, and stinking of excrement and urine. *Dear God*, he asked, *is this also your will?*

CHAPTER 3

Loud and tenacious was the knock on the rough-sawn wood door of the county jail.

"It's unlocked. Shove it open," Sheriff Pearson barked.

Sunday Boys stood glaring into the eyes of the county sheriff.

"I figgerd you'd crawl in here today. Let's get your bitchin' done with. I got stuff to do." Years of hostility, trouble, and harsh weather had shriveled his face like a prune.

"Zack, I'll be brief. You and I both know Sky would never kill anyone intentionally. His record is clean as a hound's tooth. No one has ever questioned his integrity."

Sunday drew a chair up close to the sheriff, his nostrils flaring as he spoke. "That arrest you made is unsubstantiated. It was night, with no witnesses. There was no reason to hold him over for trial. I've come to offer you a proposal. As you know, I've been investing in land along the Swannanoa River. The coming railroad will follow the river, making it the most valuable property in western North Carolina."

"Sunday, puke up what you come for and be gone. I got more important things to do than listen to you brag about your Yankee money."

"I shall. With no one else listening to us, I've a proposition for you. I have an excellent twenty-acre tract on the river that the railroad must pass through. There's a nice house and cleared, fenced fields, with a bold spring. It fronts the turnpike." Sunday paused, letting the explanation sink into the sheriff's mind for a few seconds.

Zack scratched his three-day unshaven beard, spat a bull's-eye at his spittoon, and wiped his chin with his sleeve.

"So the big shot Yankee has a bunch of land. So what?"

"I bought it. The deed is free and clear all the way back to the British Crown Land Grant. Listen carefully, Zack. I left the name of the purchaser open. I'll give you that property outright. No one will ever know it came to you from me. It will be yours!"

"Am I a-hearing what I think I'm a-hearing, Sunday?"

"I know you are a smart man, Zack. The only condition is that you set Sky free and press no charges. Tell the people you've determined the case was weak and you've released him. No one will blame you."

Like a released coiled spring, the sheriff exploded. "You're a-bribing me, you rich bastard. You think I'd sell out to a turncoat? You're like all the Yankees who have already robbed the South of everything they own. For a little, I'd arrest you and put you in the stocks out on the street and tell everybody what you done. Get out from here. Stay clear of me. You make one false move, I'll arrest you, or better still, I'll kill you."

As Sunday left, Zack said, "Just for your information"—he slipped a grin—"I got a witness who seen Sky murder that feller, whoever he was. The upcoming trial will be smoking, and you'll see Sky dangle. Now, be gone."

Sunday went to Attorney Chandler's office. "I tried to reason with the sheriff. I also tried to make a lucrative deal with him, but because he is so bitter and blind, he threw me out."

"Sunday, this appears an impossible case. If Zack has hooked up with one of his bootlegging cronies who keeps him paid off, then Zack keeps his liquor business covered. That man will swear anything for him in court."

"Can we request an impartial judge?"

"That is my biggest fear. We out here in the far western mountains have little influence over the powers that be in Raleigh and mid-state. I'll do my best and explore every option I can."

En route home, Sunday's mind worked like a dog worrying a bone, studying how he could free Sky. If not legally, how else?

When Sunday rolled in to Best, a crowd had gathered to hear his report, no freedom for Sky.

"We'll go bust him out," one yelled.

"The sheriff is crooked," another declared. "It's time we showed him for what he is."

"Hold on." Sunday raised his hands. "Don't do any rash things. It will only worsen Sky's condition. Trust me to find a way to help him. I ask of you one thing: pray that divine wisdom will guide me."

A stranger, scowling, walked away. Another broke from the crowd hastily, making fast tracks toward Asheville. He burst into Sheriff Pearson's office. "Them damned folks down yonder in Best are gettin' together to bust Sky out of jail." Without a thank-you, Zack tossed him a quarter and left.

Dark came. Zack was packed ready to travel. He handcuffed Sky and ankle-chained him astraddle a horse. They rode west without anyone's knowledge.

All night he pushed the horses pitilessly to the poverty-stricken Haywood County seat, Waynesville, consisting of bark shanties, lean-tos, and brush arbors. Some folks lived in mountain caves. At sunup, he pounded on the door of Creed Gamble, a slow-witted sheriff who had been influenced and carried along by hate-filled politicians. They doled him a pittance, scarcely sufficient to support life.

"Creed, I got us another reb murderer. He's for sure a hanging prospect."

"Why'd you bring him way over here? We ain't able to feed the ones in jail now."

"We've had a bustin' out threat in Buncombe. I ain't got no other choice. Trust me. We'll work it out for you." Sheriff Pearson talked faster than Sheriff Gamble's mountain ears could hear or his mind decipher.

"You keep him locked up with chains on him. This one's a slick little bastard. He'll bust and run if he gets a chance.

"I'm gonna arrange for the quickest judge we can trust and get this feller strung up. Another thing, don't let anybody know you've got him in jail."

"Yeah, but—"

"No buts about it, Creed, just hold and watch him. Now, I need a fresh horse. Them two out there is busted. I'm a-heading for Salisbury as fast as I can ride."

Zack rode directly to Salisbury, calling on Judge Alex Cogdil, dubbed by most the hanging judge who rarely lost a case. Zack explained the case and circumstances then urged the judge to come to Haywood County with a prosecutor to try Sky Boys, being held for murder.

"Judge, this here's a big one for us. The feller is from a whole nest of Unionists. They've been a flea in my ear ever since the war. If we can string this one up, it'll be a big victory for us. The case is a mite weak, but I have a witness who'll swear he saw the fight by firelight and that the Boys feller killed the man with an ax. We've got the body and evidence."

While the judge studied his itinerary, Zack punctuated, "You come, Judge, we'll take good care of you."

Judge Gamble set the trial for the first day of May. He assigned a prosecutor to collect evidence and build a case for the murder trial to be held in Waynesville.

Zack returned to Buncombe County worn out but ecstatic.

Sunday or his lawyer couldn't break the barriers to visit Sky. Circumstances and lawlessness, due to postwar confusion, forbade proper legal procedures to be enforced.

"Tony, I don't believe Sky is still in Asheville. I'd bet my bottom dollar that Zack has transported him beyond our reach."

"I agree. I'll send some trusted men to Mars Hill, Old Fort, and Rutherfordton. I might even have them get arrested and jailed on some minor charge to see if they can hear anything to help us."

Weeks passed with no word about Sky. It was an unusually harsh winter. Rivers froze over. Deep snows inhibited travel. Snow and ice clawed at the land until spring. No one found any trace of Sky. Rumors spread. Could Sky be dead? Had he been left out to freeze in the mountains?

Another prisoner awaiting spring trial in Haywood County escaped. He ran the high mountain ridges eastward, through Wagon Road Gap, over Mount Pisgah, and sneaked into Asheville, frost bitten and half starved. He happened upon a poster that read, "$50 cash reward for the known whereabouts of Sky Boys. Contact Sunday Boys in Best, N.C." A full description followed the headlines. The escapee found his way to Sunday. "I know where the man you're lookin' for is. He's in the Waynesville jail." Sunday fed the escapee, outfitted him with warm clothes, and put more money in his pocket than he had ever had. The man left riding a gift horse with saddlebags full of food.

"Tony, let's go." Sunday found waiting difficult. They made the trip in lingering cold temperature to the small crossroads town, inhabited by full-blooded mountaineers.

The sheriff's office and jail were only a boxed building of slab lumber. Winds blew down off the Smokies and whistled between cracks, giving scant protection from the elements.

Sunday and Tony burst into the shanty jail, storming the perplexed sheriff. Attorney Chandler flashed official-looking papers at the sheriff. "I demand to see your prisoner. Now!"

The bluff worked. They found Sky hungry and cold beyond belief. Barely able to talk, he had suffered hardships unimaginable. He had survived the winter eating corn pone, raw turnips, cabbage, and raw potatoes, rarely anything more. Four chains held his wrists and ankles, affording him only space to lie on a straw mat with a cowhide for a blanket. In one corner were his body wastes.

While the attorney gleaned from Sky the information he felt pertinent to build a case, Sunday was out hunting an impoverished mountaineer who would sell him hot food for Sky. He found a sympathetic woman who agreed to do so. "I will pay you well, in cash, to daily take my boy a hot meal at the jail." The woman was aghast. There was practically no money in the mountains. The people ate only what they shot, trapped, or grew from their infertile soil. "On second thought," Sunday said, "I'll pay you extra to also bring hot food to the sheriff." Sunday opened his wallet and gave the woman ten U.S. one dollar bills. "Maybe this will help. I'll give you more next time."

The poor woman was unable to speak, only nodding her head and wiping tears off her cheeks.

"Yes, sir," she finally mumbled. "I'll feed 'im well. I promise ye."

Back at the jail with a bowl of hot pot liquor and corn pone from the woman, Sky ate voraciously.

Sunday stripped himself, giving Sky his warm clothes. He wore Sky's ragged louse-infested garments home. When Sunday and Tony were leaving, Sky's last request was, "Tell Willa I love her."

As the two men walked to the door, the sheriff's next words froze them in their tracks.

"I heer'd by the grapevine," Sheriff Gamble advised, "that the trial fer your feller back thar is May the fust, here in Waynesville."

With effort to hide his trepidation, Attorney Chandler asked, "Have you heard the name of the judge?"

"Yep, shore have. It's Judge Alex Cogdil from down in the flatlands somewhurs."

The attorney quaked inwardly when he learned the hanging judge would preside.

Sunday and Tony apprehensively started home—the lawyer, pensive; the uncle, praying.

Is there a caring God in heaven? Does he care for his children? Is he working all things together for good if they love him? Does he give wisdom to those who ask?

"Whoa! Whoa!" yelled Sunday, pulling hard on the reins. "Gee! Gee!" Turning the rig, he slapped the horse to a trot back over the past three miles. Tony, discreet, asked no questions. They pulled up in front of Sheriff Gamble's office.

"Follow me, Tony. Let me do the talking. If you want to do something, ask God to help me."

Bewildered by the sudden reappearance, the sheriff was speechless. "I apologize, Sheriff, for failing to thank you for your cooperation and help," Sunday said.

"Well, sir, much obliged." The officer gave his toothless smile. "'Taint regular I hear them words."

"I know," Sunday spoke kindly, "that feeding a prisoner is heavy on your county's budget. I forgot to tell you, I hired that woman who sent food over here today to bring it daily for both Sky and you." The sheriff sat grinning as Sunday continued. "Your prisoner is the son of my brother, who was killed while fighting against the Union Army. I'm looking after that orphaned boy. That's why I'm concerned about him."

The sheriff, wearing pathetic rags for clothing, sympathetically nodded.

Sunday cautiously weighed his thoughts and measured every word. "Also, Sheriff, sir, with your permission, I'd like to send a crew of my workmen out here to add some repairs to your office and jail. I know the war made it hard on everyone here in the mountains, especially a dedicated lawman like you who often has to go without pay to keep law and order." Sunday reached and discreetly touched the sheriff's shoulder. "Will you grant me that privilege?"

"Well, I'll be danged, that shore would be nice."

"Good. Look for my men next week. I might even toss in a sack of meal, some salt, and coffee on their wagon."

Sunday and Tony left a happy sheriff, but they were somber traveling home, both engrossed in thought and planning. A not-guilty verdict seemed impossible.

Spring came, and the date of the trial arrived. The melting ice turned crude roads into muddy ruts. Yet the curious crowds gathered, listening for reports from the courts, which were held inside a twenty-by-thirty-feet, swept-out barn, the largest building in town.

Attorney Chandler took his position in the courtroom, his defense prepared appropriately. His reception was cold. It was as if his presence did not exist.

Sunday sat on the front row on a crude chair. By his side sat Willa. Although Sunday had prepared her for the setting and ordeal, she sat in shock at the poverty, ignorance, and crudeness of the surroundings around her. Fear gripped her. Sunday moved closer and held her delicate hand.

The quick selection of a jury was a charade. The jurors were questioned and seated by Judge Alex Cogdil. Each one was obviously prejudiced against anyone with leanings toward the Union.

Sky, shackled and chained, shuffled into the courtroom with a year's growth of shaggy, filthy hair and beard. Sunday's suit, eight sizes too big, hung below his shoulders and crotch. The stench of one not bathed for a year and his ghastly appearance was unsettling. Willa turned ashen when she saw him.

"Oh my God!" she gasped and fainted. Sunday caught her fall and carried her unassisted outside to the buggy. He never left her side.

Prosecutor William Rogers was a measly fellow who with farce profundity presented the case. "This defendant, Sky Boys, of Buncombe County, cheated an unknown man out of money and other possessions during a card game. In an attempt to regain his losses, he was murdered with an ax by this defendant. In an attempt to cover his crime, he threw his victim off a mountain cliff. Sheriff Pearson located the body and arrested the defendant. Sheriff Pearson has retained the stolen property for the court."

The prosecutor paused for a drink of water from a gourd dipper before calling a lone witness who gave the following account: "I wus lead'n my hoss up the mountain just adder nightfall, and I heer'd them fellers a-quarrel'n somethin' awful. I seed by the farlight them a-goin' at it a-fight'n. That feller over thar"—he pointed his finger at Sky—"conked the other'n in the head with a ax and gashed his brains out. Adder that I skedaddled away from thar. That's all I know."

In civilized society and enforcement of state and national laws, the entire prosecution party would have been imprisoned for failure to follow legal procedures. As it was, there was no law. Every argument Attorney Anthony Chandler made was overruled. Judge Gamble brought the trial to a rapid close and emptied the room to give the jury privacy to deliberate. In less than one hour, the verdict came: guilty.

"On the findings of this jury," Judge Gamble perfunctorily announced, "I sentence Sky Boys to be hanged by the neck until dead on the fifteenth day of June in the present year. This, giving the local high sheriff sufficient time to prepare a gallows. This court is adjourned!"

Sheriff Gamble was instructed by Judge Cogdil to allow the condemned no visitors until the execution. He departed immediately from Waynesville with the prosecutor.

As Sky was being escorted back to his cell, he saw a face in the crowd that stirred him to his core. He shook his head. Was it an illusion? He let the notion pass.

While the crowd dispersed, Sunday, along with Willa, still trembling from her horrendous experience, visited and paid the woman who had served Sky food.

Sunday left Willa with Tony and went alone to visit Sheriff Gamble. "Well, Sheriff, you surely do have things looking nice here in your office."

"Well, thank ye, sir. Your men did a heap of improvements. I'm obliged. I shore appreciate them extra vittles you sent along too."

"Sheriff, my boy has added considerable expense and trouble because of his incarceration." Sunday tiptoed guardedly, as if walking on ice with his approach. "I've given a lot of thought as to how I can help your Haywood County people. I've decided the least I can do is send my carpenters back out here to build your gallows.

"Why, Mr. Sunday, I think my folks would take kindly to that idea. Money is scarce in these mountains."

"Then consider it done. Also, I looked your situation over and realize the front of your building is very close to the road. I noticed you have a small spot behind the jail, before the mountain falls off steeply." Sunday eased on carefully. "The gallows would fit nicely there and be out of the way.

"On the day of the hanging, there will be hundreds of curiosity seekers out of the coves and ridges around here. In order to give the boy some privacy, I'd like to pay my last respects to him by building a board fence around the gallows, say ten feet high, so the gawkers cannot have a heyday in his final departure from life."

"Since you're a-foot'n the bill, it suits me."

"You've already met my craftsmen. I'll send them back immediately, making certain it's completed in time for the hanging. I like it out here in Haywood County. I might camp out a few times to make certain things progress to your approval."

On completion, Sunday inspected the finished gallows with the sheriff, examining the wooden frame, the crossbar, the two upright posts, the trigger release, and trapdoor. "A new rope has been ordered," Sunday explained. "The delivery has been promised on schedule."

By friendliness, sincerity, and gifts, Sunday gained access to visit Sky for a brief time, an act forbidden by Judge Gamble.

"You must listen carefully, Sky. It is imperative that you do precisely what I tell you. Ponder my words over and over again until they are etched on the wall of your mind." Quickly Sunday explained his plan before his short visiting time expired. As he walked away, he turned and reached through the bars, embracing his nephew for the first time in his life. "By the way, Willa is just fine. She asked me to tell you she loves you more than ever before."

Six weeks expired. Hanging day arrived. It was the biggest event to be seen by the mountaineers for miles around. They came on horseback, wagon, and on foot. They arrived from Canton, Clyde, and Crabtree. Some zigzagged down from the high mountains of Balsam, Cataloochee, and Cole. They meandered out from the long valleys of Maggie, Saunook, and Sunburst. Some unknowns arrived in fancy rigs from afar.

Upward of a thousand stood in front of the jail, disappointed not to see a man swinging from a noose. At twelve o'clock noon, the sheriff, Sunday, and Sky quickly walked the six feet from the jail to the fence surrounding the gallows. The silence was like a tomb. The only sound was of the creaking of the floorboards of the gallows upon which Sky stood. He stared out into the crowd, sweat dripping from his forehead.

In less than a hundred heartbeats, the penetrating thud of the dropped trapdoor broke the silence, and immediately a doctor, whom Sunday had engaged to pronounce the death of Sky, yelled thunderously, "He's dead. Cut him down!"

The huge doors of the enclosure were thrust open in view of the crowd. From a wagon hitched to two horses parked inside the fence, four of Sunday's men leaped and lifted Sky's inert body while a fifth slit the six-foot rope above the noose, leaving it dangling from his neck. The five men carried him to the wagon. They deftly lifted him and placed him into a casket, closing the lid. After lifting the casket onto the wagon, the workmen jumped clear. Sunday took the reins and sharply lashed the horses, cracking the whip above their ears. The startled horses charged forward, causing the crowd to frantically split lest the team trample them.

Sunday's entourage swiftly mounted their waiting saddled horses to follow in the dust of Sunday's wagon. Eastward they headed to the loved ones who were waiting beside an open grave to bid farewell to Sky Boys.

CHAPTER 4

Sunday ran the horses full speed to lay as much distance behind him as possible. The crowd was astonished. Sheriff Gamble stood outside the gallows enclosure, hat in hand and scratching his whiskers, muttering, "I be danged. Ain't that somethin'."

It was a mile before Sunday's men caught up to his wagon. He had carefully instructed the riders to run parallel behind the wagon in his wagon wheel tracks to obliterate his exact course.

When he was five miles from Waynesville on the east-west stage road, he slowed his horses. "Whoa, whoa, there. Ho." The wagon turned into a thicket of second-growth bushes and brambles lashing the horses to break through the underbrush. The wagon bounced over stumps and fallen limbs.

"Hold up, men. This here's where we stomp out the sign where Sunday cut off the road," the foreman instructed.

As choreographed, the riders turned their mounts in circles in the road and into the bushes to cover the sign of Sunday's exit. "All right, fellers, let's give these hosses a blow and wait for the boss."

Inside the casket, Sky was in turmoil. He questioned if he was alive or dying. He was thrown up, down, and sideways. At one point the casket turned over on its side, almost bouncing over the wagon sideboards.

Finally, Sunday reached his predetermined spot where he could turn his wagon around. The horses stood, eyes wild looking and heaving for breath.

Sunday leaped onto the wagon and pried open the casket lid. Stunned, Sky rolled from the tumbled box. "What in heaven's name has happened, Uncle Sunday?"

"Hush, boy, we must hasten—"

"But what's this around my neck? I can't get it off."

"Oh yes, let me handle that." Sunday slipped the noose over Sky's head with a mischievous chuckle. "There it is, my boy, an elastic rope. I ordered it from a magician in New York. Six feet of it stretched and was inconspicuously woven to the real rope. The real rope was left hanging on the gallows.

Sunday's ruse, now becoming a joke, lightened Sky's spirits.

"Listen to me, Sky. Heed every detail and remember it. We have no time to waste." Sunday heaved a forty-pound backpack made of harness leather. "Don't even take time to look inside now. I planned your needs to get you as far away as possible."

"Where do I go? Which way? How far?"

"See that tall chestnut tree yonder?" Sunday pointed. "That's about a half mile down Richland Creek. When you see the waterfall, hoot like an owl four times. Make a slow count to ten. Hoot again once. Then count to ten and hoot twice.

"You'll get an answer. Go straight to it."

He stood mute, taken aback, trying to absorb it all. The gallows seemed long ago, and there was only the present and survival.

"That hoot will be from Buck Standingdeer. His great-granddaddy, Mose Hornbuckle, and your great-granddaddy, Billy Boys, were close boyhood friends when the Cherokees lived near us in Best." Sunday, trying to make haste but, also trying to give confidence in the one whom Sky was to entrust his life for many days hence, continued. "Our granddaddies and daddies were all close friends, as close as brothers.

"Buck was among those Cherokees rounded up by the U.S. government when he was age seventeen, or there about, and was one of those in that infamous Trail of Tears. That's what many are calling it these days. He and his cousin, Goliath Chickalili, escaped and returned to the Smokies. Since they returned, our family has taken wagon loads of food and necessities to his small tribe over the years.

"In order to find you, the old man who led me to your cave arranged for me to contact Buck. He has sent his cousin Goliath ahead to blaze the trail for you to follow. They will keep you off all main roads and foot trails. Lest you be seen and recognized, you'll travel only animal trails in high country until you reach Chattanooga. Buck will leave you there. Then, you will be on your own. Buck's English is broken, even crude at times, but you can understand him. Head for Texas, due west."

While Sunday was laying out the plan, Sky was shedding his filthy jail clothes and donning a new shirt and britches made from deerskin. He covered his bare feet with a new pair of shoes.

Sunday helped him shoulder his heavy life-pack. "Inside this pack is a long, detailed letter for you to follow. One more thing, I almost forgot. When you were taken from Best by Sheriff Pearson, you dropped a folded piece of cloth. It has a small bit of amber curls enfolded. I assume it has meaning to you." A smile lifted the corners of his mouth. "Willa asked me to give it to you and tell you that you are the only love for her life. She will live or die waiting for you.

"Sky, look at me. We have all prayed for your life and safety. Has God failed you yet?" Sky shook his head. "Nor will he! Trust him with all your heart. He has promised to work all things together for your good, if you love him. Let's see how he works this out. Now be gone, my boy. Follow the sun. Trust your Creator to fulfill his purpose for which you were created." A tear found a groove down Sunday's furrowed cheek. "Oh, Sky." Sunday pulled from his pocket a leather pouch. "There's some loose money here. There's more in the backpack."

Heaving a deep sigh, Sky turned, adjusted his backpack, and walked down the owl-hoot trail to meet Buck Standingdeer.

Unbeknownst to Sunday, two men had crawled through the underbrush and witnessed the exodus of Sky from his casket and his departure downstream.

The two men had been among the last to jump aside from the fleeing Sunday and his backups. Inebriated and curious, they hopped astraddle two unattended horses and fell in behind the dust cloud, holding back far enough to remain unseen. They managed to escape sight of those diligently working to cover Sunday's detour and turned their horses off into the woods.

Tying off the horses and with enough liquor to embolden them, they eyed each other. "Let's go see what's agoing on here." They saw more than their muddled mind could quickly grasp—a dead man suddenly resurrected. Frozen by what they were witnessing, the two laid low and out of sight.

Sunday turned his wagon and clicked the team back to the main road. After the crew departed, the two snoopers heard a loud thump in the wagon and then Sunday's rapid departure eastward.

Shocked, the two sat staring at each other. One found his voice enough to whisper, "Do ye reckon that cheap liquor we drunk was pison? I just seed a ghost. I swear I did, a real haint. I ain't never going to drink no more of that rotgut. God in heaven, forgive me."

By the time the two men returned to the horses they had made off with, they were cold sober. Back in town they drew aside an itinerant preacher from the lingering crowd and pled, "Please, Reverent, pray for our lost souls and pray that we won't drink no more hooch."

The following day, Waynesville was abuzz with questions. Gossip was rampant. The two drunks, after a night's sleep, had more questions than anyone. "I think we might ought to tell the sheriff. I'm kinda think'n it actually happened."

Down at the sheriff's office, the more articulate one spelled out what they had witnessed at Richland Creek the day before.

The sheriff knew the two men were notorious drunks. "Fellers, you'uns was drunk yestidy. How's why do ye 'spect me to believe a yarn like athat? Git outa my office 'fore I lock ye both up fer lyin' to the law."

The fact was Sheriff Gamble, even if he did think in low gear, couldn't get the story out of his mind. He ran the events by his wife. "Do you s'pose that fancy Sunday Boys pulled sumthin' over on us?"

After an hour of spittin' and whittlin' and trying to untangle the complexities of events during the past two days, he told his wife, "I'm agonna ride over to Buncombe and run this tall tale by Sheriff Zack Pearson. They owe me a bunch of money. Maybe I kin collect some of it while I am thar."

Sheriff Pearson was still prancing over his triumph in the hanging of Sky Boys when the Haywood sheriff rode in and reported his story.

"Are you daffy, Gamble? We all seen the man, deader'n a doornail. I'll tell you what let's do—just to satisfy your mind, we will ride down to Best and see for ourselves if they are pulling somethin' over on us."

When the two lawmen rode into the graveyard, there before them was the fresh grave with dirt mounded over it and flowers in abundance spread out.

"See thar, Gamble, even a tombstone with Sky Boys's name on it. That rich Sunday Boys didn't miss a thing. He even ordered the marker in advance. He is some big show-off, ain't he?"

As they were leaving, two weeping women carrying cut wildflowers walked to the grave. They tenderly placed them on the ground and whispered a prayer.

Darkness was not far off. The sun was spinning a golden mist over the land. Sky was in a daze. In addition to the backpack, he felt the entire world was on his shoulders.

As he stumbled along, he recounted the events of the day. *At noon I stood on a gallows. When it was tripped, I fell into space that seemed eternal. I had readied myself to enter the gates of pearl.* Then came the unknown voice. "He's dead, cut him down."

Another voice, "Move fast. The four of you, hurry."

Another shouted, "Lift him. You there, slice the rope. Go easy. Throw that rope inside. Close the lid on the casket."

Then came the Stygian blackness. He asked himself, *Did someone say* casket*? Is this hell, the place of outer darkness?* All he could feel was the rumbling, jerking movement of the casket on the wagon, and the only thing he heard was the crowd screaming. *Are those the weeping and wailing and gnashing of teeth?*

After the months of hunger, cold, and loneliness of the jail, now this, Sky concluded, *I must be insane.*

Sky's footsteps were weak, stumbling along with effort to stay erect.

He shuffled blindly. How far, he knew not; then he slumped to his knees over a fallen log. *Father God*, he prayed, *refresh my memory of how you have ordered my life. I was born in the backwoods among poor people. Daddy was killed in a hopeless cause; our log house was burned by Bushwhackers, my kinfolks murdered. You, Father, gave me a hairbreadth escape, sheltered me in a cave, and sent Uncle Sunday to take me in and establish me in a good business. How good you are, God.* Sky's new leather shirt was now streaked with tears.

Heavenly Father, I'm grateful, but my faith is being stretched mighty tight right now. When I looked at my body while I was changing clothes, I was little more than bones. Sky shivered when the remembrance returned. *Pardon my questions, God, but why those days in jail for a crime I didn't commit? Why the ruthless terror of hanging?* He paused and meditated.

Yes, God, I forgot. You were with Daniel in the lion's den. I read it in your book. When the three Hebrews were thrown into the fiery furnace, your Son was in there with them. Now I remember how you brought the end result to be for their good.

Forgive me, Lord, but I feel like your people must have felt when they stood on the Red Sea shore with an army posted to capture them. When all their hope was gone, at the last moment you provided a way for them. Sky lifted his hands heavenward. *I'm asking you to open a way for me. I have no idea what lies ahead, but I hereby place my trust in you.*

When Sky stood and opened his eyes, he saw the giant chestnut tree. "*Whoo, whoo, whoo, whoo…whoo… whoo…whoo…*"

He held his breath. He saw the water falling in the Richland Creek, and from afar the owl hoot floated back. It was Buck Standingdeer. As he approached, he was graceful as a deer. His appearance displayed the strength of an ox and the movements of a panther. He walked with the power of a bear. It was born in him and developed in the mountain wildness.

Sky's footsteps quickened. The embers of faith were fanned, and the flame of hope blazed.

He watched the figure running up the Richland Creek trail. "Sky?"

He forgot the Indians were not demonstrative, and he threw his arms around Buck notwithstanding.

He was an archetypal Cherokee Indian, with a thick chest and straight shoulders carrying a large neck the width of his head. He had the classic hawk-bill nose and dark eyes. There was no hair on his face, nor was there an ounce of fat on his small waist and narrow hips. His mountain carriage was animal-like, giving the air of knowing everything around him.

Tired but inquisitive, Sky wanted to talk, having spoken little in his months of incarceration.

"How did you learn to speak English?"

"Not good. Some. Look my lips. Watch hands. Indians speak signs."

"I've already picked up on that. I've understood all you've communicated so far."

"William Thomas, all white man. Blood brother, yes. Buck lived with Little Will. Help Indians much.

"He teach his tongue me. Teach Bible." Buck touched his chest. "He, in me, God. Great Spirit. Jesus Christ, here. I his now. Someday sky home." He pointed upward. Buck labored to make Sky understand.

"Why are you not in the western lands with the Cherokees that were driven out?"

"Buck with them. Buck run. Goliath Chickalili, cousin, run with me. We come back. Hide. White man, no see. We come home. Your daddy"—he pointed at Sky—"food to us or we die. Boys bring food. Owe life, him. Owe life, you." Buck interlaced his forearm and hands with Sky. His eyes fixed on Sky's face. "Buck leads Sky. You be free. Owe Boys life." He pointed to himself. "No Boys, no Buck."

He stood. "We go now. Much far. Maybe bad law come."

Buck agilely shouldered his bag, fixed his bow and quiver handily, and then picked up Sky's backpack. "Sky go far. Bag heavy. Buck tote pack now."

They walked until the sun slipped behind the Smokies. The day had been a long one, and Sky was weary, unaccustomed to walking for many months.

The blazed trail led them to a prepared camp. Kindling and wood lay in a fire pit for the night. A bladder of water awaited them. "Goliath here. For us. Eat. Sleep. Sun come, we go." After eating some jerky and dry berries, Buck took two snares from his carry-all, some dried apples, and disappeared into a thicket. When he returned, he rubbed his belly. "Maybe rabbit. Maybe 'coon next sun."

"Buck," Sky asked, "where on earth are we going? Tell me. I can understand you."

They both sat cross-legged, Indian-style. Buck frowned then sighed deeply. "Sunday send old man. Say need me. Tell me Sky need help. Or die by bad law. Ask Buck lead Sky to"—he struggled for the word—"Ten-see."

"How do you know where to go? I've seen no road, only forest."

"I show Sky next sun. Sunday say me, 'Goliath go.' We go way Goliath go. He make trail. We walk his way. We go old trails, deer, bears, elks made. Way Indians go. White man no see. Goliath go first." Buck pointed the westward trail. "See blaze on tree? Our sign. Goliath go…Ten-see. Make trail." Buck took his stone ax hacked the bark off a tree. "This sign, we follow."

Buck waved his hand and arm in an arch forward. "This way Buck. Goliath run back to Smokies. To Oconaluftee, home. Now free. Many die, west. Buck take Sky, Ten-see. Same trails."

For the first time Buck flashed a smile. "Sunday give me, Goliath, Henry Rifleguns. Many"—he studied—"bangs. No Indian got. Sunday say, 'Shoot, shoot, shoot. No stop.'"

He flashed ten fingers once, then five, fifteen rounds of ammunition without having to reload. Even Sky hadn't seen this newest repeating rifle. "Buck,

Goliath go back." He pointed east. "Sunday give rifles. Big medicine.

"Now sleep." Buck pointed to a bed of pine needles Goliath had raked for them.

Come daylight, Sky did not wake. Buck, knowing the exhaustion of Sky from the rigors of the previous day, allowed him to sleep. His snares had no squirrel or rabbit but rather a young bobcat. This would provide good meat for the day. It was cooking over the fire pit when Sky roused. He stood, unsteady at first. He rubbed his eyes. He scratched his belly and went to the bushes.

"Sky sleep. Long time. Good."

"Yeah." Sky was embarrassed. "Uncle Sunday would call me lazy."

Buck made a circle at his temple with his forefinger. "Not know word. Big white man word. Sky walked far." He pointed behind them. "Sky rest." He pulled a hind leg from the spit. "Big rabbit. Good meat." He resisted telling Sky it was a bobcat.

Sky wolfed the tender meat and reached for more. "That's the best rabbit I ever tasted."

"Uh, big rabbit." Buck fished for a comment, which eluded him. He was amused at the trick he played on his friend.

Midmorning they were up and moving, having covered every evidence of their having been there.

"Buck show Sky trail." He pointed out the blazes on trees made by Goliath's ax, unobservable to any but a woodsman's eye. "Follow trails, old trails. Indian walk over. White man not know way."

Sky showed fatigue. Buck stopped beside a spring. "Stay. I go." Shortly he returned with his gourd filled with berries and ginseng roots. "Berries good. Ginseng all good. Eat. Make body strong."

Bit by bit Buck conditioned Sky for the long unknown journey ahead, the mountain lore, shelter from fierce weather, food, and, above all, secrecy, at least until they left North Carolina. Together they relived mountain memories long forgotten.

The mountains were high, steep, rugged, the Nantahalas shadowing the south and the Snowbirds spreading her ridges on the north. On their remote trails, few signs of civilization existed. They went wide and shy of Sylva and Bryson where the chances of a hunter or fugitive might see them.

Sky wanted anonymity, but he knew if they were detected, Buck would silence forever the person who might expose them. His bow and arrows were always ready for use. Sky never doubted his allegiance to him, but he also knew Buck had no love for the white man, the ones who had ripped asunder his tribe.

"Sky, listen." The flow of a small creek stopped Buck. "Come. I show." At the stream, he unrolled a ball of sinew, which he had taken from deer carcasses. He tied one end to a hook he had carved from bone and the other to a six-foot sourwood sprout. "Buck fish. Show Sky." He rolled a log over and caught worms from the decay. "Come. Slow." Easing in the shadows, he put an earthworm on the hook and let the line swing over an eddy and then dropped it. *Flash*. He drew in a nice speckled trout. "Buck supper. Sky do."

Sky missed the first and second, not having the rhythm, but on the third, *wham*. “There’s my supper. Let me catch another.”

With a frown, Buck said, “No, Sky. White man take what he do not need.”

Sky learned a lesson he never forgot. Take from nature only what you need.

The trout was satisfying, seasoned to taste by some chestnuts buried in the ashes and a few berries gathered along the way.

“This. Sky.” Buck gave another hook and line as a gift. He patted his chest over his heart and touched Sky’s chest. “Uh.”

“Dark come soon.” Buck dug a platted sinew cord from his lean bag of necessities. “Show how snare rabbits.” He showed Sky how to find the faintest small game trails and how to prepare and set the snare loop and add bait. “Rabbits eat, night. Next sun, we come.” Surely enough rabbit for food the next day. Buck gave a snare to Sky.

“Sleep time, Buck. I’m pooped. Let’s turn in.”

On the morrow, Buck led Sky into the scariest place he had ever been: the Nantahala Gorge. A five-mile trek from Almond to Topton, the raging Nantahala River roared over giant boulders every foot of the way.

“Place, much danger.”

“Why dangerous? Doesn’t this trail keep us out of the water?”

“Big danger, big lights in sky.” Buck made a zigzag with his hand. “Booms up river. Big, long rain. River narrow. Water, up fast. Look up there, Sky, high up.

Waters that high. Wash ground off high rocks. If storm, we run fast. High ground. High. High. No stop. Many not fast, they die."

Sky had the all-overs listening to Buck trying to impress the dire danger of these gorges in a sudden lightning and thunder storm. He realized he could not get that kind of death out of his mind.

"Let's hurry, Buck, and get out of here." Hurry they did, and when they crossed over Topton, Sky was totally spent from adrenalin rush.

They ate some jerky, and Sky settled for rest until sleep time.

Buck kept sniffing the wind like a hound. Without explanation, he hit the woods and disappeared. Sky took advantage of needed rest for the next hour or so.

Buck, unheard, stepped out of the forest carrying a chicken, plucked and cleaned. From a bag, he produced several hen eggs, a few freshly dug potatoes, carrots, and turnips.

"Buck smell farm from people downwind. Buck take eat. Buck, Sky need. Cook bird. Eat next sun. Still far we go."

"Buck, your English is improving. You'll be a guide and interpreter for the U.S. Army before long."

"Humf, die first. Let God guide sombitches."

Seeing Buck's agitation at what he meant as a joke reminded him of an event well remembered and oft repeated in the environs of Asheville. A large, well-equipped Union brigade was marching from the plundered city of Chattanooga through the Smoky Mountains to likewise devastate Asheville. Because the Union had mistreated the Indians in the Trail of Tears and otherwise, Buck devised a plan that many say saved western North Carolina from the destruction many southern areas had suffered.

The Asheville Brigade was only a pittance and would never have been able to repel the approaching army coming through Soco Gap at the head of Maggie Valley. The army camped in Maggie for the night.

Buck, shrewd and vengeful, organized his small band of defenseless tribesmen. He stationed two and three at different sites on the mountains surrounding the valley. They had gathered wood for large fires. When darkness came, at an arranged signal, the Indians lit the fires and began shouting and screaming their war whoops.

The Union Army, thinking themselves vastly outnumbered, turned back to Tennessee and never invaded Asheville and western North Carolina.

Mountains diminished to hills made travel easier for Sky and Buck. After three days, following Goliath's markings, Sky began to hear a roar that shortened his breath.

"Buck, is that a waterfall I hear? Sounds like the Nantahala River again." Sky was obviously shaken.

"Ocoee River. Big. Mean."

"Can we go around?"

"Not go. Chattahoochee Mountains there." He pointed south. "Ap'lac'ans on north. Must go Ocoee Gorge. Sky camp here. Rest. Next sun, go. Sky pray. Buck pray. God do best."

Sky did not sleep well. He dreamed of the Nantahala River, storms, and people running to higher ground as the river quickly swelled and devoured them.

They entered the gorge on the north side, unable to cross the river's untamed spume. It's roaring raged even more than the Nantahala, which Sky hoped he would never experience again.

The deep gorge with high cliff walls on each side obscured the towering masses of thunderheads. Then it came, like Satan himself had unleashed it. A bolt of lightning cracked below them, and the jagged streak danced the middle of the river, by them and out of sight. It was followed by an ear-splitting blast of thunder. An immense cloudburst had formed up river in the Blue Ridge Mountains, and a wall of water became a roaring torrent.

Buck raced beside Sky. "Must go high." However, the mountain behind them was sheer and forbidding. Buck pulled Sky to a massive entanglement of fox grapes, the main trunk, two inches thick with branches a century old had grown high up the cliff, digging her roots into the crevasses of rocks.

"Climb high, Sky. Fast."

Buck was frantically seeking another vine to climb. The first he found gave way, dropping him to the start. The waters were already to his waist, bearing great logs on its crest. He fought to stay afoot. The rolling wall of brown water rushed at him. As it swept by, it entangled Buck whose mighty strength was impotent against the raging flood. He grasped at a nearby branch, using all of his strength to hold on. Buck roared, using all of his strength to hold on, but the flood was stronger. A large rush of water slammed into him, and he lost his grip. The driving fury of the flood took him under and away. Great streaks of lightning lashed at the darkened mountain. Sky was dumbstruck.

"Buck! Buck! Are you there?"

There was no answer.

The flood didn't respect the loss of his friend and continued to climb higher, threatening to give Sky the same fate. Sky managed to secure his heavy pack and inched higher, his hands and fingers holding like a steal trap. Pulling with his arms and his feet seeking footholds to push him along, he came to a ledge ten feet or so above the water line, which seemed to have reached an apex. However, hail continued to beat upon him.

Dark fell. The diminishing sound assured him during the night that the waters were receding.

Come daylight, Sky sat high above the river on a ledge and never felt so alone in his life. His trusted companion was gone. No doubt Goliath Chikalili had likewise perished.

God, Sky prayed, *you saved me again, miraculously. I'll follow and trust you.* Dark fell, but there was no sleep for Sky during the night of roaring water. He heard the sounds of objects racing below him. Gigantic boulders rumbled along the river bed, at times crushing and grinding together like millstones in a grinding mill.

The loss of Buck hung heavy on Sky as he reflected on the one who perished trying to save his life.

Dawn came. The storm rolled and grumbled like an old man snoring in his sleep. Now he could see the devastation that had taken place during the dark hours. An outhouse tumbled end over end. Bodies of deer and bears bobbed up and down in the churning waves. Sky lost his composure as the corpse of a man facedown, arms spread, came into sight and then vanished downstream out of sight. Tears washed his cheeks when all he could do was pray. He heard the sound like a bass drum before it came into sight. From around the river bend above him floated a copper liquor still; its copper shined like a penny.

A giant pine tree precariously leaning over the river finally gave way to the undercutting of the rushing water. Sky saw it coming, afloat, the top limbs sweeping the mountain wall on which he sat. He pushed as far back into his cavity as possible, holding fast on to his backpack. The end limbs brushed him but passed over without snagging his clothes.

The thunder prowled in the gorge, growling like a bear with a toothache.

Toward noon, the sky began to lighten as the final edges of the storm passed, allowing the sun to break through in patches. Gradually the waters began to recede. Sky carefully eased back down on the grape vine and began walking westward.

CHAPTER 5

Hungry but too afraid to stop and eat, Sky set a gait to take himself out of this deep valley of death. Around him the mountains were high and steep. When the sun passed overhead, it was gone again in less than two hours.

He found a gigantic chestnut tree that had its roots washed from the soil by the flood waters and had fallen across the Ocoee. He held out his arms to balance his steps as he crossed to the south river bank.

Within an hour, he found a blaze that Goliath had made on a tree. He followed the faint game passageway on a trail less followed. His thoughts turned often to Buck, especially when he ate fresh rabbit and fish caught with his snare and hook.

He pressed on, always westward. The loss of Buck was a constant sad memory. However, loneliness was his greatest enemy. Being away from Willa, unable to touch her and hear her voice, tempted him to throw caution to the wind and return to her. Reality reminded him that to return was suicide and would also expose Uncle Sunday for the ploy in his escape.

He had to silence the inner voice in his head and continue on to a new country and a fresh beginning. He realized he had no other choice.

As he continued to follow Goliath's marked trail, he began to smell an odor unfamiliar to him. It was similar to that of a decaying animal corpse yet distinctly different. He recognized the main road ahead and took his usual precaution to listen and watch for human passage. As he crossed the road, careful to leave no footprints, the odor intensified by the breeze blowing into his face. When he had gone about fifty steps, he saw a tree, standing higher than those around it.

The source of the foul odor was hanging about five feet above the ground. A half decomposed man's body hung with a rope around his neck. He could see a large note attached to the decaying body. Curious, he circled to put the wind at his back and ventured close enough to read the handwriting, which appeared to be written by an illiterate person. It read, "Dam Yanke Sint to Hel."

Memories flashed back. Horrors of the hate-war when he was younger, his own father, a casualty of blind prejudice, and his own escape from the noose flooded his mind.

He needed shoes, his own worn and exposing his feet to the ground. However, he didn't have the heart to remove the dead man's shoes. He moved on.

He stood on a hill about a quarter mile from the road near the hanging man. He heard baying hounds in the distance. He knelt behind a bush to watch the road and remain unseen. Before long he saw a man appear running, as if for his life. Closer now were the men obviously tracking the fleeing man. Four men, each carrying long guns and two others holding the leash to a pair of bloodhounds, appeared momentarily then passed out of sight.

God help that man, whoever he is. Help him reach the Ocoee River and throw those dogs off his scent. Even if he drowns, it's better than the noose.

All day Sky followed the trail marked for him. At times the trail led around rock bluffs that reached out over the murderous river. At long last, the terrain began to change from steep mountain to rolling hills. He breathed the scent of fertile farmland as opposed to scent of acid soil under hardwoods, laurel, and rhododendron. The horizon ahead was clear blue, leaving behind the never-ending mist of the Smoky Mountains. There was not the humidity that existed in the valleys that were shadowed from the sun but the open warmth of sunshine that began to enliven his spirits.

Sky began to pick up the faint sound of a child in distress. He digressed from his hidden trail to investigate the source. As he neared, he realized the cries came from the main road running east to west. As he approached, he saw a man unsuccessfully attempting to lift a wagon off a child. The road circling a hillside had become waterlogged by the recent flood and had given way on the downward side. The father and son were thrown off, but the upside-down wagon had pinned the child's leg under its sideboard. The mule had been pulled off its feet and was lying likewise helpless, entangled in the harness rigging.

As desperate as Sky was for non-recognition, he knew he had no choice but to help. The boy's leg was not only broken, but the bone was sticking out the flesh and bleeding. Without a word, Sky ran to the wreckage and found a pole to use as a lever. He yelled at the frantic father to carry a huge stone to the wagon for use as a fulcrum to place under the pole.

"Grab the boy under his armpits and drag him out!" he shouted to the hill man who was standing befuddled and looking on.

He screamed again trying to shake the confusion from the helpless man. "Dammit, man, pull the boy out!"

The father jerked as if slapped and ran to the pinned and wailing child. The man pulled as Sky strained.

The child was free, but the blood loss was great.

"Jerk off your shirt, man. Give it to me. Move. Quick!" He used the shirt arm sleeves to tie a tourniquet around the child's thigh.

"How far are we from your home?' he asked the father.

"T'aint far, a mile er two down yonder."

"Is there a doctor anywhere nearby?"

"Ain't no doctor in thirty miles from here. In Chattanooga. I ain't never seed a doctor."

Sky, to bring the man out of his daze, went to him, grabbed him by his shoulders, and shook him violently. "Listen to me, man. Listen. That boy's going to die here in the woods if we don't hurry. Now, you help me find two stout pieces of wood about two feet long. Look that way. I'll look over here."

Sky found a dead tree and broke it to a proper length. The man shouted, "I got anothern!"

Sky looked into the pitiful eyes of the lad. "I know the pain is bad, son, but I've got to stretch your leg and get the bone back under the skin. It's going to hurt very much. You can cry and scream all you want to, but it's got to be done." The child blinked and nodded weakly. Sky rolled a rag and put it in the boy's mouth to bite on.

"Man, sit on the boy's chest, facing forward. Hold him at all costs. He will fight you wildly. I'll pull his leg back into place as best I can and tie these two poles to hold it in place." He cut four two-feet-long straps from the mule's lead lines to secure the splint. The pain was agonizing, and the child screamed and tried to fight his way free. The lad soon lost consciousness from the pain, which was a great help.

Next, he and the father unhitched and untangled the mule and got it on its feet. They laboriously righted the wagon, hitched the mule again, and got the wagon back on the road.

"Let's load the boy and take him home. If you know how to pray, ask God to help your son. Only a miracle will save him."

Before sunset, the two men and boy rolled into the yard of a dilapidated shanty. There were four crude walls of poles tied together with slabs for a roof. Brush stacked against the sides helped turn the wind.

The man disappeared without warning, leaving Sky alone with the boy and his mother, who was too shy to talk.

Two hours later the man returned with a pound of ground cornmeal. With scarcely anything to eat in the house, the man had taken a poke of corn to a tub mill, which served five or six other families, and slowly ground the meal by hand. The woman baked the food in a Dutch oven on the hearth and poured some pot liquor in a wooden bowl for him. The man and woman spoke little but insisted he sleep over for the night.

Next morning he finished eating the corn pone and ate a raw turnip.

"How's the best way for a person to get to Chattanooga from here?"

"Jest hit that thar road and keep humpin' it west. I ain't never been to no big town, but that's what I heer'd others say. I ain't never seen no outlanders either 'cept you. I jest see folks in this here holler and that mountain over yonder."

When Sky departed, the boy was still unconscious and was very hot with fever, but Sky knew he could do no more and bade them farewell. He slipped a fifty-cent piece in the man's hand, probably the first money he had ever possessed.

Seeing that Sky was traveling afoot, he said, "I'll sell you my mule fer 'nother one of them moneys. I can swap fer 'nother mule."

"I'll give you two more coins for a blanket, bridle, and some grain to feed the mule."

The man's toothless grin portrayed that he thought he was suddenly rich.

Sky likewise felt it was a gift from God to have transportation for the final thirty miles to Chattanooga.

As he approached Chattanooga, he passed over Missionary Ridge. The road was lined with cannons left behind when the war ended. Hundreds of graves marked only by wooden crosses were everywhere. At the first crossroads on the town's edge was a general store with a sign pointing to the rear of the building. "Haircut: 10 cents, shave: 10 cents, bath: 10 cents: hot bath: 15 cents." He availed himself with his first bath, shave, and haircut he had taken in weeks. He had long ago begun to smell himself. Inside the store he saw his image in a mirror and could not recognize himself.

"What's your name, mister? Where you from?" asked the barber.

He had failed to choose for himself a new name. His first thought was of the first president. "It's George Washington, from up Virginia way," he lied.

"How much farther to the middle of Chattanooga town?" he queried quickly.

"You're nearly there now. Just follow that road. You'll get there soon."

The destruction of the town was unbelievable. Both the Blue and Gray had fought to control Chattanooga. Thousands had died at Ft. Oglethorpe, Lookout Mountain, and Missionary Ridge. The residents had lost everything, many living in the open like animals.

A snaggle-toothed woman in gaudy red clothes adorned with cheap baubles held a sign: "I do anything to get food for my younguns." A half mile farther, a young woman, he judged younger than he, spoke to him with kindness and pled, "I need sumpum fer food. I'm hungry."

Touched, he handed her a twenty-five-cent piece and asked her where he could buy a suit of clothes.

"Down yonder on Market Street I reckon. I never been there. You want I should go with you—I'll show you."

"Thank you, no. I'll walk down alone."

On Market Street, he inquired about a clothing store. Once found, he walked in and announced, "I want a suit, a shirt, tie, and a pair of shoes. I also need a travel bag."

His present garb obviously drew sarcasm.

"Those items will cost a lot of money. Do you have cash?"

He took a chance, pointed beyond the door, and offered, "My mule there, I'll trade him for my outfit." The offer was not uncommon, since money was exceedingly scarce and barter was common in the economy.

The merchant, knowing he could sell the mule for more than the value of the clothes, shrewdly said, "No, but if you'll toss in one dollar to boot, I'll trade."

Sky countered, "I'll give fifty cents, not a cent more, and you'll have to sew the duds to fit me."

"Deal." The merchant grinned.

He stepped behind the curtain to change his deerskin outfit he had worn for weeks and donned his new suit. On second thought, he wished he had offered his old leather instead of the fifty cents.

He had rolled his leather pants and shirt around his worn shoes and walked out buck naked for measurement and to wait for the tailoring. The merchant said, "I can use those deer skins to make gloves. I'll give you one dollar for them."

"I don't know about that," he responded, trying his best to act uninterested. "I tell you what I'll do. I'll wear the leather while you tailor my suit. I'll go eat a bite, and you think over a two-dollar offer while I'm gone. I'll sacrifice that good Indian tanned leather for two dollars."

For the first time since he left Best, he felt excitement and freedom.

He gorged himself with a steak, potatoes, beans, and hot bread. While he ate, he watched with compassionate eyes the passing of people, the look of despair in their eyes, and children picking up crumbs from the ground to eat. He wondered to himself, *Was that war worth all this misery, not just here in Chattanooga but in towns and cities across the country?*

After his meal, he returned to put on his new attire. Nothing more was said about the leather, the merchant possibly hoping it was a forgotten matter. However, Sky picked up his leather and headed for the door.

"Whoa there, I almost forgot. Here is a two-dollar bill for that deerskin."

"I changed my mind," Sky shrewdly countered. "I think I'll keep them."

"Now hold on there, a deal's a deal."

"True, but you didn't seal the deal until I was leaving. I think I'll keep my leather clothes to work in."

The merchant-trader started to speak, trying to reopen the negotiation, but Sky stepped in verbally. "A good trade is one where everyone is happy. I'll make a deal with you, if it will make you happy. I'll give this good leather outfit for that beaver hat hanging on the wall." He had previously tried it on for fit.

"Oh no, that hat was imported from England. I had to pay more than two dollars for it."

"Okay, no hard feelings. I don't need a hat anyway. Good day."

He had walked about ten steps up the street when the merchant came running up behind him carrying the hat. "Here, fella, I've decided to swap with you. Take the hat."

Sky Boys had walked into a new world. In his new outfit, a bath, haircut, shave, carrying a new grip into which he had packed his valuables, he walked along the street erect and confident. Gentlemen tipped their hats and spoke when passing. He remembered Uncle Sunday speaking of such respect and recognition during his business days in Europe and New York City.

He secured a hotel room. His accumulated exhaustion had caught up with him. Inside his room he fell across the bed and slept. He did not move his body from well before dark until the sun was two hours high the next morning.

As he stepped from the hotel, he heard a deafening noise followed by a loud swish. "What was that?" Sky turned to the innkeeper in surprise.

"Why"—he chuckled—"that's the train preparing to leave in an hour or so."

Trying as best he could not to display his ignorance, Sky probed, "Where does the train go today?"

"To Nashville. It's the best transportation these days. It's nearly done away with wagon freighting these days. Quicker and cheaper."

"Does it haul people to Nashville?"

"Not yet. Probably in a year or so. Just cargo now."

Curious now, Sky said, "Reserve my room another night."

He took two steps at a time up the staircase to his room.

He was breathless with excitement as he opened his bag and took out Uncle Sunday's map. From Chattanooga to Memphis, staying due west, it looked to be about six hundred miles. He realized his exhaustion from his past two hundred and fifty miles from Best, North Carolina, to Chattanooga, Tennessee. He began to figure on a better way—the train.

He had never seen one of those iron horses, as many were calling it, so he walked the quarter mile to the railroad yard. He stood fascinated looking at the monster, sitting at idle, puffing and huffing like nothing he could conceive to compare it to. He walked the length of the five cargo cars, trying to figure a way to mount the monster for the trip to Nashville. Maybe from there to Memphis. *Perhaps*, he thought, *they'll carry passengers on into Memphis.* But for now, Nashville was his aim.

For information, Sky looked up a saloon. Loose gossip was always rampant there. He didn't take long finding the Choo Choo Tavern. He ordered a shot of whiskey to carry around, imperceptibly spilling the contents to fake consumption.

"Any you fellers ever been on that train to Nashville?" Sky asked.

"Been on it? Heck, I shoveled coal on it fer six months 'fore they fared me."

"I'm killing a little time. Let's you and me have a drink—on me."

"I got all the time in the world, 'specially if'n it's free likker. I'm perty dry today."

"Go over to that table in the corner. I'll buy us a bottle."

"I'm a headin' thar now. You hurry back." The fired railroad man licked his lips as he moved.

"Give me the cheapest bottle of liquor you have, bartender."

"Well now, that'd be moonshine. It's thirty cents a quart." He set a quart jar on the bar.

"Keep the change." Sky laid a fifty-cent piece down and picked up two glasses.

"Thought you'd never git chere." The prospective informant turned the jar up to his lips and glugged three swallows before catching his breath and shaking his head. His eyes shined with tears as the hooch burned its way down.

"This train to Nashville?" Sky asked and pulled the fruit jar over and placed it on the floor beside him. He didn't need a drunk's fabrication. "What time does it leave Chattanooga?"

"She pulls out in the morning at eight bells sharp rain er shine. 'Cause of the mountains twix here and Nashville, she chugs sorta southwest to git 'round the mountains, 'specially Lookout, then she'll light a rag northwest for Nashville.

"Say, feller, whatever yer name be, gimme 'nother snort of that joy juice, will ye?"

"Go easy on this. Here, let me pour you some in a glass. You can take the whole bottle with you. Let me ask you something else. You're a smart man. I can't imagine why the railroad let a wise guy like you go."

"Well, ya know—"

"Excuse me. Let me ask, if your mother was sick and dying in Nashville, could you find a way to ride that train. I know they don't usually haul passengers."

"You're right on that. They caught a few trying to steal a ride, and they throwd 'em in the calaboose."

"Yeah, but you're a wise man. I'm saying if a smart man like you had to go, and not get caught, what would you do?"

"Since you put it that way, I'd go down yonder, right at the Georgia line where the tracks swing 'round ole Lookout. There's a hump there steeper'n a mule's face. Ole pokey chugs pert ner to a stop 'fore she tops the grade. There's one bend near the top where a curve hides the engine from the caboose. If'n there's room at all, you can jump in the boxcar. But you be careful. Don't ye stumble and fall under the wheel. And if'n they nab ye, I never seed ye in my life. Can I take my bottle and go? I'm running late to see a feller 'bout a dog."

"One more thing. How can I know the best place to jump off when we reach Nashville?"

"Oh, that's no trouble. The engineer will blow the whistle three times. They'll stop her a few miles this side for the switchman to change tracks. It's brushy 'round thar. Jest jump off. You're on your own, buddy. They'll catch ye if'n they can."

"About what time does the train top that steep hill at the Georgia line?"

"Oh, 'bout one thudy, I'd guess."

"Thanks for your advice, wise man. Here's your jar."

Sky looked up the livery and engaged conversation with the owner of several rigs.

"How much would you charge to take me to the Georgia line where the railroad curves around Lookout Mountain? I have business there."

"Business, thunder, 'taint nothin' thar but wildcats and rattlesnakes. I'll take you thar for ten U.S. dollars, but you bring along some vittles."

"I'll meet you here at daybreak, ready to go." Sky gave him a modest deposit with the promise of full payment when they pulled away.

He went back to the clothing merchant. "How much would you give for my old leather suit?"

"Five bucks today, and I don't have time to haggle."

"No deal, but I'll give you a real bargain today. I'll trade my new suit for my old suit, backpack, and a pair of gloves."

The trade was made. Sky promised to bring the new suit back when he changed. The merchant trusted him. Being a man dealing with people every day, he sensed this man could be trusted.

Back at the hotel Sky repacked his belongings in his old, weather-beaten backpack. He squished his expensive hat flat on top. He kept loose bills and change for tips and bribes and secured his derringer, a small pistol, above his right wrist.

As promised, Sky returned the suit. He returned to his room apprehensive but anxious to face tomorrow.

At sunup, Sky, wearing his old leather pants and shirt, was at the livery.

"Are you ready to go, Capt'n?"

"Readier'n you. Hop on." Sky had purchased for each of them a fist-sized biscuit with ham and some apples for a midmorning snack.

Sky said little, but the driver wanted to talk.

"That yonder is the east end of Lookout Mountain. Thar"—he pointed—"that's Chickamauga Battlefield. In all, they say the war kilt over fourteen thousand men within ten miles around Chattanooga. Most of the people didn't know what the hell they were killin' each other for. That's the sad thing."

As they approached Wildwood in the northwest corner of Georgia, Sky saw the steep grade he wanted. Giving no explanation of reason, he spoke, "This is it, partner. I'll leave you here. Take the extra two-dollar bill and buy your kids something they need."

"They need a mighty lot," he said. "I'm plumb obliged, feller, and I wish ye well." He turned his wagon and headed back eastward.

Sky had arrived early to check everything out. He found the curve that would hide the engine from the caboose where, at a slow speed, he could swing aboard.

The plan worked. He ran and jumped into a boxcar with space enough in the load for him to squeeze himself and his pack.

Before dark, he heard the whistle. Once, twice, and thrice. The train began to slow. He shouldered his backpack feeling certain this must be Nashville. He watched for a hidden spot where he could jump, unseen. He leaped. It worked. He laid low in the bushes for two hours waiting for the train to reload, make a turn around, and head back to Chattanooga.

"Hold on thar." Four men had Sky surrounded. With his pack, it was useless to run.

"What chyou doin' on railroad property?"

"I'm walking to town. The bushes are so thick I found it better walking on the tracks." The men had no uniform or identification, so he followed his hunch. "I'm going to visit my dying mother. Let me slide this time, and I'll never bother you again. I'm going to lay some U.S. currency between the tracks. That'll help you and let me move on."

The men looked at each other, and Sky walked. When he was out of sight, he lit a jack, hit the woods running, until he broke into the open population. As in all post-Civil War ravaged towns, the houses were crude. Many dwellings were tents, abandoned by troops after the war. Everywhere he looked, poverty stared him in the face. He walked on, doing his best not to attract attention. His mountain clothes allowed him to blend in with the less fortunate.

He was brutally tired after running from the four men whom he figured were bums, trying to extort money by whatever means they could. The emotional grind of playing hobo, knowing the consequences if he had been caught, were wearing on him. He walked wearily into the town of Nashville.

His goal was Memphis and the Big Muddy he had heard so many tales about. In his mind he could hear Uncle Sunday saying, "Follow the sun, boy. Head due west for Texas."

Yes, Texas. After that, only God knows what.

CHAPTER 6

The Nashville Hotel sign seemed to spread its arms and beckon Sky Boys, the fatigued traveler—the man on the run, the man fleeing for his life.

In the lobby, he jingled a bell, which drew the attendant from behind the curtain separating his own quarters.

"A room, please, one night, maybe two."

"That'll be a buck, in advance. It has a bowl, a pitcher of water, soap, towel, and thundermug."

He shed his pack and pulled out his packed clothes. "Can you get my shirt ironed and my suit whisked and pressed and up to my room at daybreak? How much?"

"Twenty-five cents. My wife will leave them at your door. That's a quarter in advance."

Sky laid a dollar bill and a quarter on the desk.

"Name, please."

"S—" *Oh my soul*, he caught himself. Weak of breath because of his unconscious lapse of memory, he said, "George Washington. First name's Sidney, but I go by George. From Virginia. Just passin' through." Then he quickly asked, "Can you suggest a place to get supper?"

He was directed to a rooming house owned by a widow who cooked for her roomers. In spite of his efforts to use the manners his mother had taught him, he ate like a fox hound—the first meal carefully prepared for hungry working men since he left home.

The hungry roomers ate without conversation, their day's labor displaying their exhaustion. Sky, hungry as he was, ate slower, and he was left alone at the table. A second helping of dessert was placed before him from behind his back by the smooth hand of a young woman. He caught a vague feminine scent as it passed.

"Thought you might like a second." The voice spoke softly. "I baked the pie."

To George, who had not seen a pretty woman in over a year, the face hovering one foot over his shoulder was fascinating. She moved her well-developed body back a couple of steps, cocked her head slightly, and smiled. George turned and saw a beautiful young woman. Her chocolate hair, chestnut color eyes, and soft alto voice ignited a fire that mingled with adrenalin, racing through his body. An angel could not be more beautiful than the face that was three feet from a man in his prime who had not seen a pretty woman since he went on the run months ago.

He sought words. There were none. He could only look. She smiled.

"Mama said she bet you'd like more sweets."

"Yes, but the hand that delivered it and the smile is better than the dessert."

"You are some flirt, you are. But I don't mind. Sit still. I'll get you some more coffee." She took his cup, walked to the kitchen, and George felt goose bumps ripple across his skin as her five feet, well-proportioned body disappeared into the kitchen. She stuck her head, with long, flowing, shiny brown hair framing her smiling face, around the doorframe. "Cream and sugar? Or black?" Her voice was soft and eyes expressive.

"Surprise me." He swore to himself that he heard a faint giggle.

Was she an angel or human? She broke his thoughts with quick, light steps and placed a cup of sugar with a puddle of coffee on top. One of the few times in his life, he was stumped. He looked at the cup and then slowly up at her. She broke into a hilarious giggle.

"Surprised? You asked for it."

For the first time in over a year, he experienced hilarity.

"So I'm some flirt, am I? Well, hello, you're a big tease." She was experiencing a rush throughout her body of gaiety and freedom that seemed overwhelming.

Her mother appeared with a cup of hot coffee with a touch of cream and sugar. It appeared obvious that the mother was in on the joke.

"We are so fortunate to have you visit our home," the mother announced. "Will you join us in the parlor for a visit? The table and cleanup can wait. We have so few visitors, and we'd feel honored to have you."

He felt embarrassed in his month's old Indian-made leather suit, knowing he must have a foul odor. "I apologize for appearing in these leathers. I've traveled many miles and have not taken time to change. The hostelry is pressing my suit for tomorrow."

"Fiddlesticks, take no thought of your dress. We see working men every day. You are dressed well compared to some of them."

Mother, daughter, and George moved to a small sitting room, and the mother touched a match to the wicks of two lamps.

He realized the pair of eyes had not shifted from him. When he turned to look, her face was flushed, her eyes wide, and hungry lips parted slightly into a smile.

"I'm George Washington, from Blue Ridge, Virginia." He didn't know if there was such a place, but it sounded right, and from that day, he felt he was a new man with a new name.

"I supposed you were from the Appalachian Mountains by your woodsman suit. Buckskin, isn't it?"

"Yes, ma'am, but I have better."

"So, George Washington, what brings you to our town?"

"Mamma, you've fussed at me for asking strangers questions. And, Mamma, could George and I visit alone a little while?"

"Of course, and George, forgive my inquisitiveness. We have so few visitors, I guess I got carried away."

"And what, ma'am, is your name?"

"Apologies again. I'm Helen Robertson, and this is my daughter, Patricia."

He stood immediately. "I am glad to meet you both." He sat and the atmosphere became more relaxed.

"Mamma…"

Helen took the hint and began cleanup chores in the kitchen.

Patricia was not shy. She moved closer to George, sending his mind into a whirl. He had been away from feminine contacts far too long for a young man his age. He fought for inner discipline, but his hormones were ablaze.

"Trish, may I call you that? How has a lovely lady like you dodged the hordes of suitors?"

"Yes, George, you may call me that, and have you not noticed there are very few men my age alive in Nashville? Tennessee seceded from the Union, and the Confederates made Nashville a stronghold. The Union Army came en masse to defeat the Confederates. In doing so, they destroyed our town." Patricia was beginning to tremble, and her chin quivered. "In the major battle, twenty thousand Confederates were killed and fifty-five thousand Union fighters died." She paused. "My daddy, my two brothers, and most of my kin were killed. I'm sorry, George. I don't want to talk of the war. I just want to talk to you. You are the first man I have talked to face-to-face in months." She wiped away her tears and eased closer to George. "Now do you understand?"

Her story reached into George's heart. "My daddy was also killed, and every member of my family except one perished."

George quickly remembered, *Don't say too much. Don't leave a trace. You're on dangerous ground here. Step away.*

"I'm sorry to hear of your loss, George." Patricia reached over and touched his hand, giving a gentle squeeze. "We have so very much in common, don't we?"

To George's relief and good fortune, Mother Helen had finished her work and rejoined the two who were tiptoeing to the brink.

Seeing an out, he stood. "It is late. Most folks are in bed by this hour. I must catch the train tomorrow and move on."

Patricia looked startled. "Can't you stay—another day?"

"You have a great life ahead of you, Trish. I will pray for you and all the things you need for happiness." His eyes turned to Mother Helen. "Thank you for this evening and for bringing such a wonderful woman into the world."

Sky walked to the door, fighting back his own emotions and memories.

In his room, George Washington had a battle with his inner demons. He was a new person now—outwardly—but the love of Sky Boys and Willa was as fresh as life in this moment. In bed, he tossed; he hugged his pillow. He squeezed it in his arms, hugged it, and lay on top of it. *How can I extinguish this fire burning inside me?*

He remembered. He lit the lamp, dug into his pack, and pulled out the small folded corner cut from Willa's dress. Back on his bed, his hands carefully unfolded the treasure. His fingers took the tuft of curled hair Willa had cut just for him and lifted them to his nostrils. His body exploded in release. It was as if she were there—her unique scent, her touch. He held Willa in his memory, the one who set the standard of womanhood by which every woman he would ever know would be measured.

But how? How can I reunite with this woman who carries my soul? Reality again slammed the gate. He could not return to Best. *She doesn't know where I am or if I'm alive. Oh, God,* he prayed, *make a way for Willa and me to have a life together, a home, and a family.*

Fatigue overtook him, the inner tension had escaped, and he slept.

At daybreak, he heard a gentle knock and knew his clothes were ready.

He dared not eat breakfast at Patricia's house. He fought off the temptation. Instead, he ate at an establishment near the train station.

"A ticket to Memphis, how much? Can I go today? What time?" He patted his lapel to be certain Willa's folded treasure was secure, the only thing he had of her except his memories.

A short toot of the steam whistle commanded attention for the all-aboard announcement of the conductor. Curious, George was like a child, and he was the first to go up the train steps into a new part of his world. The plush seats, fancy lights, lace curtains, adjustable shades, polished hand rails, and hardwood flooring grabbed his attention. His head was on a swivel as he walked down the aisle, taking in every gadget and furnishing. A small door in the rear tweaked his curiosity. He opened it to the sight of a convenience he had seen in everyone's yard back home—an outhouse, except it was indoors. Visible, looking through the hole and four feet below was the stone-covered ground, cross ties, and track. Sniffing, he thought of all the human waste scattered across the country by the travelers. The walls were set with tile, and the single seat was made from a slab of polished granite with a large oval hole. *Why didn't I think of that in advance?* It would be quite a long wait from Nashville to Memphis. The world was surely different outside of Buncombe County, North Carolina.

When the seats were all taken, except the one beside him, the passengers quieted to a scene taking place at the front entrance of the train. A man, accompanied by a girl child, whom George judged to be four or five years old, began with great effort to mount the coach. The well-dressed man had only one leg, and the train, designed primarily for bipeds, presented difficulty in the man's negotiation. George immediately perceived the problem, rushed forward, and hefted the man by putting his shoulder under the armpit of the legless side and easily lifted him to his seat. The young girl carried his crutches. With prolific thanks, the man insisted that he accept a U.S. five-dollar bill.

"Under no circumstances, sir. My daddy would reach down from heaven and kick my backside if I didn't help someone in need." To quiet the man's insistence, he took the money and handed it to the child and returned to his seat, with the one beside him still vacant.

A buggy sat at the curb. The woman inside it had witnessed the loading ordeal of the crippled man. At the last moment, two men carried a trunk and two suitcases to the storage in the baggage section following the passenger car. The men returned, escorted a woman to the train, and George saw her give each a gratuity that made them smile and tip their hats. She instructed them to give an additional tip to the buggy driver.

The conductor escorted the lady to the seat beside George. He quickly stood as he had been taught.

The train blasted its definitive toot, and the eight-car train began its groans and squeaks as the engine began its *whuf, whuf, whuf, whuf* southwestward to Memphis.

The conductor stood, swaying to the trains movements, and pulled from his vest his gold, double-case Elgin. "Ladies and gentlemen, we are leaving Nashville on time." He studied his watch with a look of grave importance. "It is exactly ten minutes past ten o'clock." He snapped the cover and replaced the timepiece carefully. "We should arrive in Memphis about five forty-five"—he chuckled—"unless we are forced to stop for a cattle drive. The rope overhead in the center of the aisle can be pulled for an emergency stop, only, may I emphasize, only in case of emergency." He bowed as if he had quoted Shakespeare and disappeared behind a door in the front end of the car.

George attempted to organize his composure to address the elegant lady in the seat beside him. The faint aroma of perfume was affecting his masculine equilibrium considerably, and the aura of her nearness threw his thoughts out of kilter.

The train was now rolling at the speed of a fast-walking man when the little girl walked from her front seat to the toilet, which was behind George's seat. She entered and clicked the door latch. In less than five seconds, a violent scream erupted followed by a desperate cry. "Help, help, help me!"

George sprang with automatic reflex, kicking the door from its bolt. The child had sat on the polished granite. Her small body had slipped, bottom first, through the hole. She was clinging to the rim under her armpits and her legs bent at the knees, frantically holding on, apt to slip through and under the rail cars behind.

He yelled, "Pull the rope, the emergency rope, overhead, quick!" As he spoke, he gripped his hands around the frantic child's wrists, pulling her to safety.

"It's all right, darlin' one. You are free." He held her to himself and caressed her golden hair. "You are safe now, free." She pressed her trembling body against the one who had saved her.

The man with only one leg was crawling down the aisle, pushing through the crowd of some who had stood to witness the terrified child and the man who had rescued her.

"Everyone sit down. You there"—George motioned to a large man—"lift that man and help him up." He took the child to the arms of the man, known now to be her father. After the father and child had caressed, he carried the child, and the other man assisted the father back to their scats.

The train had stopped now. The conductor and his assistant had run to the scene, but not before the situation had settled. All was quiet except whispers among the passengers and whimpers from the child lying in her father's arms.

Everything in order, the engineer released the brakes to allow the train to chug along to Memphis.

George sat back in his seat in a daze, exhausted. His eyes were closed in a silent prayer of gratitude. The woman beside him studied the hero, the child's savior. He opened his eyes and saw, eighteen inches from his face, the beauty of one who made him momentarily wonder if he had died and awakened in glory land. As her soft blue eyes caressed him, all he could do was smile and courteously nod his head.

"What you just did was the most valorous thing I have ever seen."

"I only did what most men would have done, ma'am."

"No, you did it with compassion. Few, if any other man, would have comforted that child with the love you expressed."

"Thank you, ma'am."

"I have watched you for the past hour while I waited in my buggy for the train's departure. I saw your respect for the elderly while others passed them by. You helped with the luggage of a mother carrying an unborn baby and attempting to control two other small children. No one else recognized her plight. You did." She paused, and George sought for a response. "You gave candy to that poorly dressed lad, perhaps the first candy he had ever eaten. You stopped to pet that mangy dog that followed you to the train."

George sat devoid of words. Yes, now he remembered those kindnesses, but they had been forgotten. To him, they were the acts that should be performed.

"I was reared to believe if a man is kind to the elderly and children, if he is kind to animals and they trust him, he is a good man."

"So…how do you do, sir. My name is Jacqueline Delmas Corn, widow of Matthew Corn who was murdered by Bushwhackers after the war."

"Accept my condolences, madame. I lost my family in that terrible conflict. I hid out in a mountain cave, having no desire to shed the blood of my fellow countrymen. My only living relative is one uncle."

"And you are from where?"

"Excuse me, madame, I am George Washington, from Virginia." He lifted his hand as if tipping his hat.

"And what, may I ask, brings you to western Tennessee?"

"I am on a mission for a time en route to Texas."

"George"—the woman's countenance turned serious—"I may be presumptuous, but please allow me to discuss my circumstances and dilemma. May I?"

"Yes, we've a long ride to Memphis, and I assure your confidentiality, and also I like to hear you talk. Your accent resembles music. You asked me what brought me to western Tennessee. What brings you here?" He used his quick question to sidestep any further query about himself.

"Oh, my accent." She gave a feminine chuckle and lifted her fingers to her flushed lips. I've tried to hide my native French. I seem to forget I have a language and speech variation.

"My late husband was a major in the Union Army, distinguishing himself in the Mexican-American War.

For his unique service he was given a land grant of three thousand acres in Locke, Tennessee, some of the most fertile farmland east of the Mississippi River. I had come to St. Louis from Canada where my parents had emigrated from France. I was young, twenty at the time, when I met Major Corn, who had recently retired from the military. He was twenty years my senior, but I fell in love and married him. He brought me to his plantation in Locke—in truth, the end of the world."

The day was hot, and the woman tapped her face and neck with her handkerchief to remove the perspiration. Her long, flowing blonde hair showed evidence of the heat and humidity. She watched the endless cotton fields across the horizon. "May I continue?"

"Of course you may. You were at the world's edge, and your husband…?"

"He established a profitable plantation, one of the larger cotton producers in the state. Then the war came. Recruiters from the north and south conscripted all the workers except the older men who could produce only light labor. With the scarcity of labor and the death of my husband, the plantation is now producing nothing.

"I am returning now from Nashville where I completed the final transactions, placing everything in my name. He had no children. I was his sole heir."

"Wait, please, madame—"

"Please, I prefer simply Jacqueline," she interrupted. "I'm all American now. All my holdings bear the name Jacqueline Corn. Please call me Jacqueline."

"Thank you, but why are you confiding these personal matters to me, a stranger about whom you know nothing? For all you know, I could be fleeing from a murder." George shivered at the thought.

"I am a desperate woman. I know no one I can trust. The war killed most of the young, able-bodied men, and I live, if not at the end of the world, you can see the end from there. I have no managerial talents and no knowledge of farming. I live there alone except for an older Negro maid and her husband who tend to my animals and do light chores around the main house. My home is their only home."

"How do you manage to live financially, if I'm not being too personal?"

"Money is not a problem. Major Corn had made good investments in northern industries that are yielding well. I need someone who is trustworthy to manage my plantation. In truth, I'm asking you to consider the job. I trust my intuition. I believe you are honest." She looked him straight in the eyes. "There is a nice house beside mine. I will deed it to you. I will have a lawyer draw up a contract to protect your interests. You will be paid liberally. If everything is not working for the good of both of us, you can leave after one year with severance money in addition to your stipend."

She paused. George's mind was spinning faster than a runaway wagon wheel.

"My carriage will be waiting at the train depot in Memphis. We can be in Locke before dark. You can look things over, ask questions, think it over, and give me your decision after a few days' consideration."

"You have shot a cannon off in my brain. Allow me to get a hotel in Memphis, clear my mind, and pray about this matter. If I do not feel divine peace, I will do nothing. Agreed?"

"Agreed. I respect your wisdom in making a decision. That's the reason I felt you were the man I needed. We are nearing Memphis. May I have my carriage driver deliver you to a hotel? Thereby, he will know where to meet you in...?"

George picked up her pause and said, "In four days. Two hours after sunrise."

George was conveyed to the Big River Hotel. Their departure was friendly, but he saw her eyes moisten as she rode north en route to Locke.

George Washington from Blue Ridge, Virginia, registered at the hotel. He felt his mind overloaded and confused. In less than a month, he had cheated the gallows and fled over one half thousand miles toward some unknown destination called Texas.

Today he was a new man with a new name, a new life, and a new beginning. Due to no effort on his own, he had been offered a job, including a home of his own and an open check by a person of wealth who stood in dire need of his services.

During his evening prayer of gratitude to God for his miraculous protection and guidance, he made one request: *Heavenly Father guide my steps. Not my will but yours be done.* Somewhere along the twisting roads of his thinking, he slept.

One important facet about the scenario that George had seemingly not picked up on—and probably the fact had not entered the consciousness of Jacqueline—was that she was a beautiful woman in her prime of life. Her emotions were defying gravity. Her loneliness and inner feminine desires were bottled up inside her exquisite body. Absolutely, she needed a plantation manager. Most of all, she needed a man.

George—handsome, kind, courteous, and unattached—prompted her to throw caution to the wind, bring his masculinity to her end of the world, and to her.

Cupid had loosed his arrow. Jacqueline was in love.

CHAPTER 7

The Big River Hotel was a doozy. Nothing had been spared at the hostelry, built since the war with no consideration of cost. It had never entered George's mind that such a place existed. He registered for two days and pulled his purse to pay. It was then he learned how such splendor could be built—and paid for. He checked out his room, left his belongings, and went for a stroll.

The crowds merging in Memphis were an amalgamation of different people: Swedes, Poles, Germans, French, British, and farther on, Russian. The men and women had risked everything, even their lives, to satisfy their hunger for freedom. They had pushed through hardships, storms, and perils at sea. Some who had been prisoners were shipped to America from abroad. Prostitutes were sent. Some arrived as mail-order brides ordered by frontiersmen because of their lack of women, who feared going to the unsettled and unknown land.

The Mississippi River, which had divided the nation, had been spanned by only a few bridges, forbidden by its width and costs. Therefore, most of the people from the southeast, heading west, made their crossing at Memphis.

George walked the streets and marveled at the people, taking in their strange customs, costumes, and languages.

As nighttime approached, the city came alive, first with dining, then dancing, and then devilment. Being unfamiliar with such activity, he chose to return to his room and called it a day.

George was up, washed, and dressed at the break of day. After breakfast, he sought a clothing store to supplement his only dress outfit. He bought a leisure outfit—britches, shirt, shoes, belt, and a cap. He looked at himself in a mirror. Sky Boys, dead and buried back in North Carolina, reincarnated now into George Washington.

He wanted to examine the big muddy Mississippi River up close, so he ventured to a game trail closest to the water's edge.

He froze. *Was that a voice?* He placed his cuffed hand behind his ear to amplify the sound. Again, a faint call for help. He thrashed through massive underbrush into the water itself. "Hello," George called. "Hello."

"Help me."

The voice was upstream. He could see a body, now caught in a tree branch growing into the river's surface.

"Hold on. I'm coming for you." He raced upstream beyond the helpless man, jumped into the river, and pulled the man free. He struggled with the man's body, pulling it to the riverbank. He laid the elderly man belly down onto the ground. He was already turning purple. Not knowing what to do, he pounded on the man's back. The man gurgled then regurgitated a large volume of water out his mouth. George, in desperation to do something—anything, slapped his open hand on the man's back again. A cough. A deep sigh. He opened his gray eyes and then closed them again.

George leaned over him near his face and said, "You're going to be all right, old-timer. Keep on breathing. Stay with me now."

He lifted the frail body in his arms and carried him about a mile to his hotel room.

As George hastened through the lobby, he called out, "Somebody get a doctor! Be quick! This man is near death." He carried him to his room, and in spite of his muddy, wet clothes, he laid him across his bed, unconscious but breathing.

George observed bulges in the man's pockets and on examination saw bound packets of U.S. currency. He put them in his suitcase for security.

Within ten minutes, a doctor came carrying his physician's satchel. He was directed to George's room to examine his patient. "This man has been beaten severely. You say he was in the river?" The doctor questioned. "I suspect he was beaten, thought to be dead, and tossed off a river boat. One thing is for sure, young man, you saved his life."

The physician cleaned and covered the man's open wounds and left medicine to make him rest, promising to return before noon the next day. "When the newspaper gets word of this, you will be a hero," the doctor mumbled.

"Please, Doctor." George subdued his panic. "I'm a private person. Let's not allow this matter to become news. I'm just a traveler passing through to Texas. Would you do me this favor and simply let me move on?"

"I shall honor your privacy, but take it from me, you are a brave person to risk your life in that murderous river. Her suck holes have dragged many a man to his death. I'll see you tomorrow."

George stood helpless over the man. *What will I do with him? Can my involvement endanger my new identity? What if the law questions me?* Also, there was Jacqueline. *What will I do about her offer? I promised her an answer in four days.* He kept fingering at his brain. He felt as if his mind was a whirligig.

It was predawn. The man groaned and then stirred. George was on his feet immediately, lighting a lamp.

"How are you? Are you in pain? There is medicine the doctor left."

"Thank you. Yes, I have pain." The man settled when the sedative took effect.

"It has come to me now," the man spoke. "I heard your conversation with the doctor." George listened with intensity.

"Day will break soon. Go out immediately and arrange for a carriage that I can lie down in. We will go to my house. I have a personal physician and appropriate help. Get your things ready. Come home with me, as a courtesy."

George packed quickly. He made no inquiry at the hotel, but outside on the street he asked where he could rent a large carriage. He ran to the place suggested and arranged a funeral carriage that could be harnessed and ready in one hour. He gave directions where to come.

George raced back to the hotel, gathered his belongings, and gently carried the unknown man to the street. George whistled the attention of the driver who parked in front of the hotel.

The hotel manager demanded payment in the lobby for extra cleanup. George paid the amount quickly and gave a liberal gratuity. He also left behind a liberal payment to be paid to the doctor for his two visits.

The man lying in the funeral carriage instructed the driver to go in the opposite direction of his home until out of sight of the hotel and then circle and head in the direction of the Bluffs.

George had never seen anything comparable to the man's mansion. His opulent home sat on one of the majestic Chickasaw Bluffs.

When the carriage came into view, two butlers and two estate attendants ran to meet the carriage.

"This man needs assistance—" George began but was cut off.

The man's attendants, seeing the need, took over the gentle handling of the man, obviously their employer. They assisted him through the front door, held ajar by a primly dressed maid.

George paid the carriage fee. The driver left, smiling with the tip he received.

The attendants addressed George as a dignitary.

"Please wait in the living room. Breakfast is warm and will be served shortly," a butler advised. "The washroom is there. Down that hallway to the outside are the facilities. Out that door is the comfort station."

George returned for a sumptuous breakfast served by two attendants.

When he had finished breakfast, he was invited to the man's lavish bedroom. His attendant was dismissed. George was invited to sit.

"My name is Franz Buechner. Welcome to my home. I owe you my life, and I am deeply indebted to you."

An attendant knocked and rolled in a tray with hot coffee, cream, sugar, and tea for Franz.

George was holding his cards close to his chest trying to avoid questions that might reveal his true identity. He had introduced himself as George Washington.

Everything surrounding him bespoke elegance. There was silver flatware placed beside fine English bone china. The rugs, he supposed, came from the Orient. He remembered the awe he felt at Attorney Anthony Chandler's house, but it in no fashion compared to the grandeur of this man's stately home. Yet he was a humble man, with no pretension and never a boast. He felt at total ease in his presence.

The mature wisdom of Franz perceived George guarding himself. He caught immediately his Appalachian dialect. He had been taught manners, courtesy, and primary etiquette. Behind all this there was caution, a barrier concealing his past and true identity.

"Mr. Beuchner, there was money in your pockets. After I had carried you from the river to the hotel, I observed the edges of currency showing. I removed them and placed them in my suitcase, lest someone else take them. If you will have my case fetched, I will return it."

Franz gently tinkled a bell signaling an attendant who was summoned to bring the case.

As suspected, the certificates were water soaked, eliciting laughter from Franz. He instructed the attendant to iron the bills flat and dry them.

"Young man, your integrity is commendable. I had no remembrance of this money. You could have kept it, and I think you know that, but you returned it. This will not be forgotten."

"Sir, I must admit, I'm not a perfect person. I have not taken a vow of celibacy. I'm not natured that way. The fire of manhood burns in me constantly. I'm not beyond lying. I have stolen when hungry, but I was taught honesty, and I try to practice it. Mainly, I feel the presence of Christ in my life, and it is my main goal in life to please my God and obey God's commandments. I wish I could say that I have always done that, but I have failed often. I am extremely glad I did not keep your money."

"Most remarkable, indeed." Franz was impressed.

"I am not a religious person," Franz confessed. "However, I do set a high standard for my life. Perhaps someday I'll feel a need for divinity." Pausing he looked as if far off and scratched a spot on his head. "For whatever reasons, I have been a blessed man. I possess far more than I deserve. I have often wondered why I have been rewarded so lavishly because my life began in abject poverty—over in the old country," he reminisced. "Opportunity came for me to come to the States, and

I took it. Having heard of the United States, I hid in a ship sailing across the Atlantic. Hunger drove me out of my hiding, and I was indentured for payment of my passage and worked for my freedom. An appetite for learning drove me to the university, but I took to gambling more than the books. After accumulating quite a large sum of money, I quit school and made a career of playing poker professionally." Franz paused as if bringing back memories.

"When the North and South began rattling swords, I sailed back to Europe. My gambling expertise rewarded me well. Fortunately, I saved most of my winnings." He smiled with satisfaction, not egotism.

"When the United States government became stable again, I converted my gold into U.S. certificates, returned to the States, and elected to move to the interior of the continent. The war had ended, and because many had lost everything, there were bargains everywhere for those who had the king, cash."

Franz laboriously stood to stretch the aching body that had been badly beaten the day before.

"I purchased the two hundred acres here on the Bluff overlooking the river to the west and the fertile farmland surrounded on the other boundaries. Through my contacts in Europe and New York, I was able to furnish it."

"It's the most beautiful house I've ever seen." George spoke as his eyes roamed the room.

"My only living relative, Uncle Sunday, lived in Europe during the war. He told me of his gambling exploits in England and France. Your story is much like his."

"Did you say Sunday? I knew an unusual man by that uncommon name. Now he was some poker hand. Not a common last name either. I'll never forget. His name was Sunday Boys."

George felt his breathing become short, heart beating rapidly, and his head lightened as if he would faint.

"Was that man large? Say, six feet or more, maybe three hundred pounds, balding? Did he say where he lived?" George fired his questions with mixed emotions.

"That description fits him. Funny thing"—Franz laughed—"he was from North Carolina. His English was spoken with perfection but with a distinct mountain dialect, not that of the Piedmont nor the eastern Carolinas, somewhat similar to yours, as I recall."

George was dumbfounded. He found himself struggling with a dilemma. *Can I reveal myself to Franz? Will he turn me in to the law if I confess who I am and my circumstances?*

Franz was expert in reading body language, eyes, and expressions. He knew he was scratching at something very deep and well concealed.

The sun had reached its peak. Franz and his guest sat before a bountiful lunch, elegantly served. George, usually hungry, picked lightly over his food, his mind trying to work out a decision.

After the noon meal, Franz took a nap. George walked the lawn around the huge house. In his mind, it was surely a castle. He smelled the exotic flowers, the freshly mown grass. He saw birds, the likes of which he had never seen. On a long pond were ducks, geese, and swans. Two whitetail does and their fawns drank from the far side of its waters, and fish leaped to the surface. A multitude of birds were singing to the universe. To George, it was an idyllic Shangri-la.

"How do you like it, my friend?" Franz called from his veranda.

"It's a paradise."

When George returned to the house, Franz asked him if he would like to play a game of poker. "We'll play for chips, for the fun of it. I like to keep my hands and fingers limber. Have you ever played poker?"

"Some. My uncle and I played some after he returned from across the Atlantic."

It was no time at all until Franz realized he was not playing a novice. He studied George's nimble fingers, watched his face and eyes, his cool manner, his frozen face bluffs, even the raking to himself his winnings. His play was a masterpiece of the game.

The hour came when tea was served. George had never tasted hot tea, and he felt shy, trying to emulate Franz in preparing it to drink. His little finger had trouble sticking out when he lifted his cup.

Franz was not fooled.

"George, a man has the right to keep his life and his past to himself. I respect that right. However, if you choose, you can share with me anything you wish. You are safe here. I swear to you my confidentiality."

The massive room settled into a long silence. At Franz's signal, the doors were closed. The room was empty except for the two. A breeze stirred the curtains as it caressed the room.

"Franz, I lay my life in your hands."

"That is all right. What you tell me will not go beyond these walls. You have my word. Hot pincers could not claw it out of me."

"My only living relative is an uncle. He is Sunday Boys, brother of my father who was killed in the war."

Franz sat in overwhelming wonder. "Sunday… your uncle?"

"Yes. When he returned to western North Carolina after the war, he found his homeland in shambles like so many others, destroyed by both armies. I hid out in the mountains and escaped death. Uncle Sunday looked me up and took me on as his son. He kept me and set me up in business." He saw astonishment in Franz's face

"I am not George Washington. I am Sky Boys." He spread out his story of the past—all of it, up to Sunday's escape ruse, his perilous journey through the Smoky Mountains, to Memphis, and to his leap into the Mississippi to drag out a drowning stranger.

Franz sat in amazement. "A coincidence like this could not happen in a thousand lifetimes."

"The last words Uncle Sunday told me were, 'Go to Texas. Take on a new identity. Tell no one who you are or about your past. Start life over again.' I can never go back."

"Well, young friend, you have told me enough. I believe your story one hundred percent. To me, your past is behind you. Gone. It will never be mentioned again, under any circumstances. I know your real name, but let's keep you George Washington." Franz was grave. "You are a long way from North Carolina. However, you dare not make a slip.

"You are protected here. I invite you to make this your home. Sit tight and sort things out. I'll be a few days or maybe weeks healing, and your company will be refreshing to me. I never had a son. Actually, I never got around to marrying. You can be my son, at least for a while, only if you choose. You are free to leave at will."

"I could never ask for more. Being able to confess to someone your mistakes, weaknesses, and sins and then to be accepted as you are is one of the greatest gifts one can receive. I will gratefully accept your invitation to stay here, at least for a time. It will allow me some thinking time, and I do need rest, in my mind and in my body.

"However, I have made a commitment to meet with someone three days from now. I will return to Memphis the night before I leave."

"I shall not cluck over you nor meddle in your affairs, but"—Franz gave a capricious smile—"is she pretty?"

George was set back by Franz's intuition. "How did he know the matter was a she?" He showed surprise.

"Since you know the life-and-death secrets of my life, I will tell you this one also. I met a woman on the train. She had been in Nashville settling the estate of her deceased husband. She was frank with me, telling me her large plantation needed a manager, and she was incapable of handling the job herself. Whether her decision was prudent or not, I promised her an answer in four days as to whether I could come look over her situation and consider her offer. I must admit she is a beautiful woman."

"Madame Jacqueline Chaban-Delmas, widow of Major Matthew Corn?" Franz lifted his eyebrows and smiled.

"Yes, she's the one. Do you know her?"

"I have seen her. Neither I nor anyone else *know* her. Major Corn married her, brought her to Locke, and they rarely socialized. Of course, he was busy running the plantation. That is about all anyone knows of her. She told you correctly. Manpower is practically unavailable since the war. I can imagine she is desperate for help. The ideal would be for her to sell out, but buyers are few, and cash is scarce these days." Franz paused, thinking.

"Major Corn himself was quite wealthy, outside the value of the plantation. One can assume she is a woman of great wealth. Go and see for yourself. This may be for you. I need not advise you to consider carefully. One's heart and one's head are difficult to synchronize in matters such as this. I admire you, George, for honoring your word."

That day, George suggested that Franz call his physician to examine his wounds.

"I shall not do that. I feel well. I do not allow outsiders the freedom to come to my house. Gossip has a way of spreading. Life has taught me the less people know about one's life and activities, the better off one is." Franz, idiosyncratically, lifted his eyebrows and reminded George, "That will be good advice for you in the future, Mr. George Washington, from Virginia."

On day three of George's visit, Franz continued to recover from his wounds, but his age slowed the process. Franz had ordered the preparation of his carriage, and he showed George the highlights of his estate. It was not a plantation but a beautiful portrait painted by God's hand including his creatures. All the seeds he planted were now the backdrop George was seeing and consisted of everything a man could desire. He had trained groomers for his animals, skilled arborists for his exotic flora and fauna, mechanics, and household attendants for every task. George's mind boggled at the mere thought of the total monetary value.

Following an afternoon nap, Franz sat with George beneath a giant oak, cooled by a gentle breeze flowing easterly from across to the Mississippi River.

"George, I have been studying you. Many traits I admire in you, and one of them is you are not a bitter, unforgiving person. Having told me your story of the hatred and injustice you have endured, you have not once spoken rancor or hatred against your enemies. That I find commendable."

"My folks taught me to forgive. They read God's book to me as a child. 'If you forgive, you'll be forgiven.' I've done my best to stick to my raising. I've learned too, when I don't forgive, it hurts me more than the other person."

"I've been waiting for you to ask me about the incident that landed me in the river, and by the way, had it not been for you, I would not be alive today," Franz admitted.

"Fact of the matter is," George confessed with a smile, "I've been curious. My folks taught me to not meddle in other people's private life. I would like to know, however. It was a bit unusual."

"I make my living playing poker on the Tennessee riverboats. If a person is good, he can make a lot of money. He makes his money off those who think they are good at card playing. Successful poker is a skill, not a game. I feel certain you have been told that before by your uncle Sunday.

"Sometimes, one prefers leisure over poker. That was my problem the day you rescued me. I had become indiscreet with a gambler's girlfriend, and we got caught together. He beat the hell out of me and almost sent me there. I suppose he thought I was dead. He dumped me overboard. There are many men's bones in that river for shenanigans like mine, and few are ever investigated."

"Uncle Sunday told me once that a man only had enough blood in his body to fill one head at a time. You've just explained to me what he meant."

After a delectable dinner, Franz challenged George to a few hands of poker. It was obvious that Franz's intentions were to give George a test to see to what extent Sunday Boys had taught his nephew to play in the serious art of the game. For only one hour they played.

They went into a suite that Franz had designed in his home for poker playing only. Franz played with all the intensity his cumulative experience of legerdemain had taught him. If he, while shuffling, ran up a top stack or a bottom stack, George froze. When Franz raised his eyes to George, all he got was a cold stare. If Franz deftly attempted to shift the cut, deal from the top or bottom, George commanded his attention with a gruff clearing of his throat or an intentional cough. After all his attempts with slick aces, marked and trained cards, George did not fail to detect every sleight of hand. To Franz's wonderment, George countered his illusion with one of his own in his next deal.

"I give up." Franz threw his hands into the air. "You've beat me at my own game. To beat all," he confessed. "You did it with poise. You are a gentleman, Sky Boys. Excuse me, George Washington. You are a copy of the man I played years ago, your Uncle Sunday. Congratulations, lad."

After the game, the two men, the elder and the youth, retired to their rooms. George made preparation for the scheduled visit the following day and took cover in his bed.

There was no sleep waiting for him. The gravity of what lay ahead of him was strong. There was no doubt that Jacqueline was serious in her offer and in her need. Franz had confirmed that. He fought to keep below the surface the beauty of the woman. Her kind voice lingered in his ear. In her eyes, he read volumes. Her age was no factor. Few women he had known compared to her beauty. However, he realized that was his heart reasoning.

What were the practical considerations? First, and always, his true identity would hang over him to his grave. Could that be preserved in Locke? His desire was to settle down for keeps and raise a family with never a worry about his past. A beautiful woman like Jacqueline would likely marry someday. Where would he fit in that scenario? *What if I marry and have children? How would that work into the puzzle?* There was the matter of truth. Could he be at peace without revealing who he really was, and if he did, would she accept it or someday hold it over his head as a threat?

When the clock was striking midnight, he touched a match to a lamp. George was a gentleman who could not bring himself to hurt or offend anyone intentionally. His decision to gently decline Jacqueline's invitation was difficult, but he felt it to be the best for him and ultimately for her in the long run.

In the wee morning hours, he, with deep emotion, penned his decline and determined to hand it to her driver to deliver it back to her.

Early the next morning, Franz was up to see him off on his venture. "My driver will deliver you to your destination. I have instructed him to make open arrangements with the public wagoner in Memphis to return you back here at any time you choose. Speaking of time, I noticed you do not have a watch. I've brought you one from my collection. I'm sure you know where I got them. I bid you farewell and godspeed."

At two hours past sunrise, George was waiting for the carriage traveling on the road south from Locke. He had intentionally moved up the road, out of sight from the hotel. He took no chance in being recognized as the one involved in the river rescue.

He was comfortable with his plan to hand the carriage driver his letter to Jacqueline, give him a gratuity, and return to the safety of Franz's estate to rest up and later head for Texas.

A carriage driven by an older Negro appeared from over the horizon coming from the north. George knew it was from Jacqueline.

He stepped into the road to intercept the carriage and confirm if he was from Jacqueline. When the carriage stopped, the door opened, and he was struck dumb. Jacqueline sat smiling. "I came so you would not be alone in your trip to my home. Get in. I have some cookies, but the coffee might be a bit cold."

Her words left him in a stupor. Not just a conveyor to pick him up, but Jacqueline, twice as beautiful as the traveling women on a train but cosmeticized and dressed, as he imagined, like the queen of Sheba.

"Get in, George. The people at the plantation have prepared and are waiting for you. Driver, let's take this man home."

CHAPTER 8

George was speechless. This scenario had not been included in his plans. His emotions exploded in every direction at the same time. He felt his mind had shut down. Then, things changed as his masculine vigor took over.

Her blue eyes were like a child on Christmas morning opening her gift. Her face was radiant as a mother seeing her firstborn. Every joyful emotion given to femininity he saw displayed in her in that one moment.

"Oh, George, seeing you now is like the second coming. I could not allow myself to send someone else to pick you up. The past three days have been agony waiting for you. Get in this carriage, and let's go home."

Home?

George had not yet said anything. First, his surprise forbade it. And also, what could he say?

"Don't just stand there, you handsome fellow. Get in, and let's go."

George, the extrovert, had in his lifetime only a few moments when he was lost for words. This one capped them all—he was baffled.

What would he do? What *could* he do?

Like a man dying of thirst, having a cup of water held out to him, he walked to the carriage and stepped aboard. As the driver turned the wagon, George realized that he too was being turned.

Jacqueline snuggled up to him like a sick kitten to a hot rock. They rode in silence—George in turmoil, Jacqueline purring as if in seventh heaven.

The carriage passed through the dilapidated, untrimmed, vine-covered gate. George realized he had to say something. "Are we on your property?"

"Oh, George, let's not talk about my stupid property. Let's talk about us. I've dreamed for years for this moment, for someone to banish my loneliness, of a living, breathing person to talk to, hold—to give myself. Let's just savor the moment."

He was in shock. *Dear God, what can I do? What are your expectations of me? There's a raging fire burning out of control inside me, and Satan is throwing kindling on to it. Now I know how Samson felt on the lap of Delilah. Help me, Lord.*

With his masculine virility stretched to the limit, he recollected Joseph when the king's wife sought to draw him to her bed, and he fled, leaving his coat in her hands.

"Jacqueline," George spoke urgently, "please excuse me." He opened the door and demanded, "Driver, stop the carriage." George ran into a copse of underbrush, and out of sight, he lifted his hands. There he confessed his helplessness, admitted his passion, and then asked, if there be such a thing as a way of escape from this temptation, grant it.

After an appropriate time, he returned to the conveyance. "Thank you for your patience. This day so far has sort of scrambled my brain. This new job offer and your surprise visit put me in a tizzy."

"Are you all right? Do you feel well?" Jacqueline expressed concern.

"Yes. How far is it to your house?"

"Just over the knoll."

"I need to walk. Are your shoes comfortable to walk in?"

"I'd walk to hell and back—barefoot—to be with you."

"Driver, stop this rig." Jacqueline was out and on the ground ahead of George.

"Driver, drive on to the stable. We will walk from here."

George kept his fidgety hands in his pockets as if feeling for something, but at the moment, his hand nearest her was free. She reached for it and didn't loosen it until they reached her home.

The house was stately but in need of much repair. The yard was grassless, however, swept clean by someone. A path to the stable and other outhouses was clear. He heard the low of a cow and the cackle of chickens. These conditions he took in with a quick glance, not daring to portray his thoughts to Jacqueline.

"Avis," she addressed her Negro maid as they stepped into the entrance hall. "My guest has arrived. Draw some cider."

The response was immediate. "Yes'm, Ms. Corn."

"George, over there is the tree-shaded side of the room. It has a cross breeze. Please sit." She wiped her face and picked up her fan. George saw another fan beside the one she took and reached for it, but she scooted a chair beside him. "No use in both of us fanning. We'll use this one to cool us both."

The maid delivered cider on an elegant silver tray.

"Ms. Corn, lunch'll be ready 'bout a hour."

Jacqueline nodded.

He sipped the cider and raised his eyes in surprise. "How did you cool this drink?"

"My late husband, God rest his soul, figured that one out. Our dug well is more than forty feet deep. He attached a bucket to a second rope that hooks to the windlass frame. We keep milk, butter, and a jug of cider lowered to the water, which keeps them cool. Avis switches the water bucket rope to the cooler bucket"—Jacqueline squinted her brow—"or something like that. I'm not mechanical." Jacqueline cocked her head and smiled at her joke.

"What a great idea. Back home..."

He did it again. He came in a gnat's breath of saying, "In the mountains, we use a spring to keep things cool."

This, along with what to do with Jacqueline, added a tighter tangle to his already-jumbled mind.

Lunch was announced by a faint bell jingle. The food was delicious, obviously prepared for a guest.

After dessert, Jacqueline told Avis to summon Wheaton.

"Wheaton, Avis, this is George Washington. He is going to be the manager of my plantation. George, these have served me well since my husband passed away. I'm sure they will serve you as well."

"How-do, suh. Pleased to meecha, suh." Wheaton bowed humbly.

"I's at yo service all de time, Mista Washington." Avis lowered her head.

"Jacqueline, I'd like to try out the double swing hanging from that huge oak limb."

The two sat silent in the rhythmic motion. The chain squeak was like the pendulum of a huge clock. Jacqueline leaned her head over onto George's shoulder.

"Jacqueline—"

"Shhh, just let me lie here and bask in your presence. Can you imagine, I have not felt the touch of a man's skin in far too long. These past few hours have been heaven on earth to me."

"Jaq—"

"Please, George, let me dip my tongue into my overflowing heart. I knew love once—at least I thought I did. I met Major Corn, and he swept me off my feet, so to speak. I was a lone young woman. He was handsome, rich, a bachelor, and he asked me to marry him."

She paused and pressed her fingers to his lips. "Please let me ramble. My heart is overflowing. Allow me to tell you the story. We married, and he took me to New Orleans on our honeymoon. He bought clothes for me. Jewelry. Everything he thought I wanted, he got it."

George could sense she was fighting tears. He waited. After a few moments, she gained her composure and continued.

"We came back here. He called it our Paradise Found. The plantation flourished during the first years. Labor was abundant. Because my husband paid top money, he rented slaves from their owners, sometimes hundreds at harvest time. He made and invested thousands of dollars from the plantation yield, in addition to investments he made while in the military."

Avis approached carrying a tray with a pitcher of cider and another of water, placing it on the ground.

Jacqueline made no acknowledgment. George thanked her, and she bowed her head as if embarrassed.

"George, I have to tell you. I think I'll die if I cannot tell someone. I am lonely. Only God in heaven knows how lonely I am. Do you know what is worse than being alone? It's being alone with someone else."

Then, the dam of tears broke, and she wept, vocally. George gave her a small rag from his pocket, and she saturated it with tears. George himself was choking tears.

"George, my husband never touched me. You know—there. After a year, I told him I wanted a child. It was then he told me he had been injured—you know, and could not be a father. He could not perform in that way to make a child. This plantation was given by the government as a compensation for his injury. No amount of recompense can meet my needs as a woman.

"I need love, George. I need you."

George felt her agony. He strove to enter into her wounded heart, to in some way feel what she felt. *God help me*, he breathed from his soul.

"Jacqueline, I am hearing and feeling every word you say. They burn deep inside me. I hurt with you. I understand your feelings. I know another widow who waited nine years for the right man to come into her life. That woman was my mamma. I've heard Mamma say time and again, 'I'm so glad I waited. I could never be happier with any other man. It was worth the wait.'"

He understandingly took her hand. "You and I have been beating around the bush about me being a manager for your plantation. What you want and need is a husband, a man who has been chosen and created specifically just for you by your creator, one whose background and education can complement your own. You need glittering candle lights, the ballroom, and theater. One who has his own wealth to mingle and share with your own."

George's breath was becoming short. His own inner fountain was spilling over. "I'm not that man for you, Jacqueline. I'm just an ordinary man from the back of beyond, a simple mountain man.

"We both have been drawn by our God-given desires like a moth to a flame, and the end could be as disastrous."

George was stretching his soul to the limit, seeking to gently handle the tender flower in his hands.

"My uncle Sunday used to assign me certain scriptures from the Bible to read every day. I memorized many of them. One is this, 'I know the plans I have for you,' declares the Lord, 'plans to give you hope and a future.'" George paused, hoping this would sink in.

"Believe me, lovely one, my life has been tested, and I've been in circumstances that seemed impossible to overcome or even live through, but I trusted God's promise, and he, in some way, met my needs. He will give you exactly your needs in a husband."

"Oh, George." Her voice was only a whisper. She had wept herself empty of tears and only choked on her words. "Could you maybe be that chosen one for me? Could we try?"

"Jacqueline, I have made one of the greatest mistakes of my life, and I've made a lot of them. I have allowed myself to hurt you. I apologize from the basement of my heart."

Dear God, how can I can I say this. Give me courage and honesty.

"I have given myself to another back over in the mountains. She is there waiting for me. She believes in me and knows I will come back to her. I cannot betray that trust. I would never be able to live with myself if I did."

Jacqueline reacted to his words as if he had spit in his hand and slapped her face. Without a word, she hit the ground running as if a demon was chasing her.

George knew he had only one recourse: run, and run fast. For about fifteen minutes of picking them up and putting them down, his lungs were hurting from his hard breathing after sprinting down the road. He heard behind him the steady clopping of a trotter's hoof beats. On instinct, he left the road and ran into the woods. The widow of a military man would surely have a gun. *Hell's fury has been stirred*, he assumed *She's going to kill me.*

The carriage stopped. "Ain't no use you runnin', Mista Washington. This here's Wheaton McIngle. I be's by myself. Ms. Corn done tol' me to tote chu to Memphis town. I lef her bawlin' her eyes out, like a caf that done lost its mammy. Sos you can come on out an lemme fetch you."

George, unsure if the Negro had a weapon or not, tentatively approached the carriage and climbed aboard. George didn't need to be told; the driver was disappointed and angry.

As they neared town, George asked Wheaton to stop the carriage. "Hold out your hand, friend. I have something for you."

"Naw, suh, you don' owes me nothin'."

"It's not pay. It's a gift." He placed in the gnarled hand a coin that glistened in the sunlight.

"Whut is zat, suh? Ain't neva seed sich."

"It's gold, Wheaton. A ten-dollar gold coin."

"Lord God Amighty, I's never had no money in all my years. Somebody'll think I done stoled it."

"No, you and Avis put it away. Someday you'll need it."

When the carriage rolled away, George could hear the man shouting. "Oh, thank you, Jesus. Thank you, Lord." The last words he heard were, "Bless Mista Washington, God. Bless 'im good."

CHAPTER 9

George began walking from the edge of town toward the public carriage service for his ride to Franz's mansion. He approached a large oak. Under the spreading shade lay an old Negro woman, her face creased and leathered as if it had worn out two bodies. Without doubt she had been one of those freed from slavery. By her side, with head pressed against her frail body lay a huge dog, a mixture of many unknown breeds, weighing at least eighty pounds. He thought as he approached her that she was dead except for a flicker of her eyes.

"Mother, are you still with us?" was the first thing that came in his mind.

"Yas, suh, jes wait'n on Jesus."

The big dog rose and sniffed his leg and then wagged his tail.

"Where are you going on a hot day like today? Are you far from home?"

"Ain't got no sich thing as home."

"Where are you heading?" He knew life was leaving her rapidly.

"I's got a boy. Folks say he live up yonder at Ms. Corn place. I jes wanted to get to see him onst again, 'fore I goes to Jesus."

"What's his name, Mother?"

"He's name's Wheaton. Ain't seed 'im in years. Wheaton McIngle."

The Negro lost strength, and her head lay to one side. The dog whined and walked to her and sniffed her face. It made two pitiful whines and slowly walked to George, looked up at him, and whined again.

He went close, lifted her hand, felt her brow, and knew she was dead.

What could he do? How could his abundant compassion help?

He left with quickened steps, heading toward central town, and he inquired the whereabouts of an undertaker. He told him the location of the body, that he wanted a casket, where he wanted it taken, and to whom it was to be delivered.

"Wheaton McIngle? We don't fool with nigger bodies, man. You ought to know better than that," the mortician spat his prejudiced words.

"Perhaps you'll make an exception. I also want you to take men with you to dig a grave and bring it at a spot Wheaton instructs you."

The undertaker stared at him, like he had eaten an unripe persimmon, but his conduct changed dramatically when George pulled from his pocket five gold coins of different denominations.

"How much, nigger hater, will it take you to become a decent human being and bury her as I've instructed?"

"Normally my fee would be five dollars for all that—"

"So be it. Since you're such a low life, I'll give you a ten-dollar gold piece. I also demand a nice wreath of flowers on top of the grave. When I follow up, the job had better be completed exactly as you've been paid."

"It'll be done as you have requested. My apologies."

"No sense in you lying, mister, with your false change of heart. You've already shown me the rot in your heart. Just be certain everything I've ordered is performed, or you'll answer to me, and may God have mercy on your evil soul."

Biting his tongue, he turned away, heading for the carriage service. He felt something touch his rear end and looked back. There stood seventy pounds of bones, stretched over by a flea-covered skin.

"Git from here, Mutt, go." He almost said "go home" but realized he had no home. "Go on. Go!" The dog turned belly up, tail between his hind legs, and whined.

"All right, Mutt, come on. I don't know what I'll do with a mongrel, but if you've chosen me, let's go. I'll put up with you as best I can. First thing, I've got to put some meat around your skeleton." He stopped by the butchery and bought a pound of meat. Mutt wolfed it down as if he had never had a bite of food. He also stopped at another store and bought some dip to kill the fleas, ticks, and mange covering the dog.

Mutt followed the carriage taking George to Franz's estate.

Sitting on the porch, as if waiting for George, Franz rose. "Welcome home, lad. I've missed you. Did that beautiful, rich woman corral you?"

"No, Franz, and with all due respect, I'd rather not talk about it."

Franz, having lived a life full of experiences, sensed that he had been through something that was embedded deep into his heart.

"It's dinner time in one hour. Freshen up, and we'll have a visit when the shade arrives."

In the cool evening, Franz was eager to talk. "George, I intentionally put you to a test the other day in the poker game. It was evident to me that Sunday Boys was your mentor. The fact is he wiped me out in London—the best player I ever sat before."

"That sounds like Uncle Sunday, but he waited a little late to teach me not to take all of a man's money."

"He told you correctly. That was part of what almost got me killed. I had done that to the man whose girlfriend and I had a tryst, and we got caught. He almost killed me. He will probably try again if he ever sees me. Some people never bury the hatchet." Franz shook his head at the thought of such hatred that drives one to murder.

"Here's a proposition I've been studying over. Let's you and me partner as a team. I'll reserve rooms on the *Robert E. Lee* steamboat. I'll hone your skills that are unique to ship players. They are the best in the world." Franz licked a stogie and struck a light, taking six or seven long puffs before settling it in his jaw.

"No need to answer tonight. Get a good night's rest. We'll discuss it more in the morning." He snubbed out the fire on his cigar and tossed it aside.

"Franz, I've a favor to ask. If I go out and bathe that dog, do you object to him sleeping in my room? I've never had a dog of my own, and he kind of adopted me."

"Of course, son, my home is yours. Does he have a name?"

"Yep. It's Mutt. He's a purebred mutt."

George dreamed of riverboats, gambling tables, and adventure until dawn.

At breakfast, George was wound tight with excitement. "The riverboat plan excites me, Franz. Let's do it. Texas can wait."

"I hoped that would be your answer. I've made a list of our preparations. Foremost is to legitimize your name. We'll appoint with my attorney. He knows the loopholes to make you Simon Peter if I grease his palms with enough money. How does the name Fritz Buckner suit you?" Franz peered out the window to hide his sly grin.

"You old fox. That's almost your name. I like it because it in some way bonds me to you."

"That is exactly my thinking, George. You are the brightest ray of sunshine to come into my life—ever. I never knew my parents. I was left on the steps of an orphanage at birth. I stayed there, strapped by rules until age thirteen. I left and began drinking from the wells of life, maturing quickly. I'm not proud of many things I've done. I've kept plenty of lubrication on my pole. I've stolen when I was young, hungry, and desperately lacking funds. As you said you had done. I've eaten many a turnip and grass. To those who cheated me, I cheated them. I've cleaned a few out of their money. Yes, I've fed a body or two to the fish in that hungry river, I'm sad to say. By shrewdness and good fortune, I've never been in a jail." Franz paused in his recollection as if hearing a voice from afar or perhaps from within. "Our lives are similar in many ways.

"There's something about you, George. I sense an inner presence in you. You always speak about a God who has led you and protected you. From the snippets of your young life, it appears there has been a divine leader. I've never before had any leanings toward religion, but your life has caused me to think about those things."

"Franz, I don't know what it's like not to trust in God. I just plain and simple believe he created me. I believe his Son came and died for my sins, which are many, because he loved me. I have never had a moment when God has failed me, even when I've failed him. I've been in some tight spots, but he brought me through them. God has used every bitter experience to lead me to trust him more. I believe Jesus Christ died on a cross to pay the penalty for my sins and that I am forgiven. That belief has given me hope, not just in this life but for eternity."

George was conflicted. He liked to discuss his faith, but he was itching to get on with the prospects of gambling.

"Franz, the truth is, I feel a bit guilty talking about poker and gambling. I can't explain that, but I do. However, right or wrong, I want to pursue this idea and see where it leads."

"That's another thing I like about you. You are honest. I object to dishonesty in a person."

Franz was beginning to act like a new man. His age was slowing him, and his recent beating was evident, but he seemed as anxious as George to launch their new venture.

To George's advantage at this moment, the Civil War had left the legal system in such disarray that people thought many were alive who were dead, or the opposite. People were translocated. Family records and documents were destroyed. The change from the bogus name George Washington to Fritz Buckner appeared to be a simple legal feat. His name was no longer Sky Boys or George Washington, but Fritz Buckner. Leaving the lawyer's office, George, now Fritz, joked, "Franz, I sure hope God keeps up with my names."

Next came the wardrobe, three of everything, triple in formal wear, including ascots and ordinary, man-on-the-street wear. "I'll explain the different sets of wear later. You'll need tie tacks and flashy jewelry, but I've scads of those. Guess who I got them from." Franz gave his familiar twinkle in his eyes. To hold his clothes and other needed accessories, Fritz bought three large suitcases of fine leather and a handbag of superior quality.

"Nothing announces success like the appearance of success," Franz advised.

En route home, Fritz wanted to stop by the butcher shop. "I gotta get more bones for Mutt. I'm getting attached to that dog. I hope he knows me by my new name."

"You and that mongrel! You're the only gambler I know who has an eighty-pound varmint and adding on pounds every day."

"I'm only a wannabe gambler so far, Franz."

Each day the two bonded closer, the old man and the boy; to Franz, a twenty-one-year-old was a boy, a boy to whom he owed his life. He was a boy more mature than most men, in his physical stature and now even in his emotional development. Franz, a man with the snows of many winters behind him, with few friends male or female, had lived a lonely existence.

"The *Robert E. Lee* is the monarch of the Mississippi. She's a beauty. They say she cost two hundred thousand dollars to build. That's ten times the construction cost of my house here. Remember, we'll depart one week from today and go to Memphis and then return. There is much I need to teach you, so listen carefully. You already know the basics, but riverboat gambling is a far cry from what you have been playing. I'll teach you and have you ready.

"First, carry a deck of cards with you every waking minute. Riffle them, cut them, and memorize the patterns. Remember the last card you see as you cut. Know where every card is in the stack. Teach your fingers to think. Be able to shift them, deal them, throw them, even inconspicuously hide one in the deck and know where it's hidden. Make your hands, fingers, and eyes all work together in harmony." Franz was packing it in. His behavior had become serious. "You will be facing men with a lifetime of gambling experience. You've heard the term 'dead serious'? Quite often the games turn deadly. Excuse me, I forgot. You already know that." That statement grabbed Fritz's attention and made him shiver.

"Always remember, henceforth, poker for you will not be a game."

Franz's brow was no longer relaxed. "Fritz, you've proved to me that you know how to play poker. Your uncle taught you well. But now I'm going to teach you a whole new way of playing the game. The style poker played on the riverboats and from here on out to California along the frontier is called five-card draw. It's not like your match or straights and pairs."

Fritz became apprehensive and anxious. "A new game? Different rules?"

"Yes, my boy, but you know all the fundamentals. Some gamblers call it not five-card draw but simply *bluff*. Etch that word on your brain. The key is to bluff. I've studied you playing, Fritz. You have what it takes."

In Franz's card playing room, the two spent hours, far into the night, learning five-card draw or bluff.

At 4:00 a.m., Fritz became weary, and sleep began to nudge him.

"From tonight on, we'll work from dusk 'til dawn. Get used to that. Sleep and recover during the day. We play all night, and our minds must be fresh."

During the day, Mutt interrupted Fritz's sleep with licks to his face. When the sun set, he stumbled out of bed drowsy.

Fritz, along with one of the younger men in Franz's employ, played a search-and-find game with Mutt. One would drag an object along the ground and hide it. Mutt proved early on to have a superior sense of smell. He even developed the ability to track one of them a mile or more. That became Mutt's game of choice.

Midweek, Fritz began to change his circadian rhythm. He and Franz even began to play for keeps. It was Fritz who challenged Franz for a head-to-head square-off for real money. Fritz lost the first night, broke even the next, and got lucky the third. When things were about even on the fourth night, Franz called it off.

"Fritz, I have no doubt you can hold your own. Let's let it rest now until next Monday when we board the boat."

Loading up for departure faced a problem Fritz had not foreseen: leaving Mutt. "You cussed dog, stop looking at me with those sad eyes and drooped ears. I'll be back." Still, if a dog could cry, Mutt did. Fritz did too, only when no one saw him.

Franz, knowing the system, had made reservations and paid in full to reserve the appropriate rooms and a large security vault. Fritz, a mountaineer, having never been exposed to the atmosphere he was now in, had innumerable questions.

Franz was patient but told him to simply follow along. Questions would be answered later.

It finally emerged from Fritz's mind that the *Robert E. Lee* was a floating gambling establishment, albeit not by name. Former abuses by sharps and sharpers, mostly dishonest gamblers, had turned gambling into confidence or con games. Craps was banned because of gaffed equipment and had precipitated laws against such and were moderately enforced. The professional gamblers, that is, those who played five-card draw, all knew each other and knew the protocol and abided by their unwritten code.

Gambling was done informally, mostly in secret and by invitation only. The gambling fraternity discretely managed and benefited from the transient nature of the riverboat lifestyle. By keeping his eyes open, Fritz soon observed that the gentlemen not only had their own organization going but the sisterhood had their own association active as well, but it didn't involve cards.

Everything that Franz had arranged fell into place. The large room was set up for the purpose of bluff. Word spread quickly among passengers who boarded for the sole purpose of gambling. Each gambler had his own sources and methods of securing their clientele.

Franz, now relaxed after getting things set up for business in their room, suggested, "Let's walk around and get a feel for the environment. You must be completely calm when you sit down at the table."

Franz knew practically everybody. He courteously introduced Fritz as a visiting friend.

"Naturally the gamblers play against each other when there are no passengers available to play. Those are dead-serious players. They'll have all the money Sunday stashed away in your backpack before you can spell Mississippi if you're not careful. Beware."

While making their rounds and chitchatting with acquaintances, Franz and Fritz rounded a corner and came face-to-face with a man who looked at Franz in utter alarm. Tense and face ashen, he turned and walked away.

"That, Fritz, is Lyndon James, the man who thought he had killed me and threw me overboard the day you found me."

"What will he do?"

"Time will tell. I wouldn't put it past him to hire a black leg to finish his job.

Fritz looked at him, perplexed.

"I forgot to tell you of a small group of thugs who travel these riverboats known as black legs. They are feared in that they are not skilled with gambling but are available for hire to murder. They kill for money."

By the second day, Fritz's adrenalin was flowing, and he was feeling cocky. Franz sat back and watched his protégé work. Fritz played with cool precision. In less than an hour, the unknown passenger had enough. "I gotta quit now. I've only enough money left to get home on."

"Thank you for the game," Fritz spoke kindly. He received no response.

Word spread about the *kid*. His reputation circulated among the pros. In turn, each took him on. Each got a taste of the innate skills passed on by way of France, England, and New York. He not only had a reputation; he had respect.

Only once did a sharper try to pull a cheat. Fritz saw it coming as well as Franz and the other professional gambler. What would he do? In abeyance, Franz held his breath. Fritz's face turned, as if to a block of arctic ice. The cold gaze into the eyes of the sharper froze him. Fritz's eyelids never blinked once. He simply gazed a glacial scowl. His opponent sat hypnotized by the fierce glower. Weakly, the sharper was able to stir and said, "I forfeit." He left his money on the table and disappeared.

As if nothing had happened, Fritz looked around the crowd. "Gentlemen, anyone up to a game?" Murmurs spread softly, but no one felt the urge.

"Gentlemen, if you will excuse me, I think I'll retire for the night."

Before he left the room, Franz had sat, and others were gathering around him.

Fritz slept until lunchtime, dressed, went to the buffet hall, and ate hungrily. To himself, he reflected, *This work is harder than freight driving in the mountains. Freighting doesn't pay as much though.*

Then she came, interrupting his thoughts. Willa. *Will I ever see my darling again? I'd give all the gold on this ship, if it were mine, to hold her today.*

"Excuse me, handsome, could we share a pot of tea?" Fritz sprang to his feet courteously, a manner he had been taught since childhood.

"Of course, ma'am, of course." A lovely looking lass she was, twenty years old, Fritz guessed, and well assembled.

"Are you on vacation, ma'am?"

"Not ma'am, silly, I'm Elizabeth, known best as Libby. I've heard your name is Fritz, and you've made quite a name for yourself. I'm a working girl myself. Would you like to spend some of that easy money for some pleasure? You will not be disappointed."

Fritz was caught off guard. Yes, he had some easy money. Yes, he had some free time. Yes, she was a pretty female, and she smelled good—and his sexual urge was up and coming.

He looked into her eyes, and her experienced eyes were burning into him.

"Would you please pour another bit of tea, Libby? Do you have time to talk a few minutes?"

"Well, my time is valuable. Time is my stock in trade. Quickly, speak up."

That was all he needed. Reality brought him back from the edge of falling into the abyss, becoming like a bear getting a taste of honey and not able to stay away.

"I-I-," Sky stammered, "I can't. I'm sorry."

While he paused collecting his senses, the fizgig, only a nymphet who had sashayed up to him, now stomped away bruised by rejection.

Dear Jesus, you know I can't take much more of this. I am trusting you to keep me true to you and pure for Willa. I know she waits for me, but will I ever see her again?

In a far corner of the room sat a group of men showing evidence of waiting to enjoy the festivities and the possibility of a card game but without knowledge of how to approach it. Fritz rushed to his room, redressed into his common duds, rearranged his room, and returned to the group, who was feeling rather loose from their midday imbibing.

"Would you fellers like a game of five-card draw? If so, I'll oblige you."

"Hell yes, we've been looking for a game."

"Let's mosey to my room, and we'll give 'er a shot."

The hayseeds fell in line. Once in Fritz's room and their chairs turned around to lean on the backs, each pulled out a role of Confederate bills.

"Sorry, gents, you had better save your Confederate money in case the South rises again, but until that happens, it's gotta be gold or United States government-issued money."

"Shucks, we was just testing you. Looks like we're stuck with this Confederate stuff. Don't worry. We got some change and a few U.S. dollars."

Fritz played them along, mostly to give them the pleasure of winning and boosting their ego. After an hour, he realized he had other duties and expeditiously relieved them of their doubtlessly hard-earned cash.

"Thank you, gents."

They left with sour-looking faces.

Fritz and Franz met for dinner together. "Well, Fritz, how do you like your new profession?"

"I like it. Like you said, I have to stay on my toes and keep my eyes wide open all the time."

"Have you made any money? You know that's the name of the game."

"Have I made any money? I've made more in the past twenty-four hours than I've made in my entire life."

"Don't get cocky. Every gambler on this boat wants a piece of you." Franz chuckled. "They'll each take their turn. You're quite a topic among the big boys. As far as anyone knows, you're the youngest gambler to play the river. Sooner or later you'll hit a losing streak. The deck shows no favorites. When those times come"—Fritz nodded solemnly—"you'll either bluff your way out or take your losses. So be ready for it."

"Yes, sir. Thank you. I needed that."

A frail man was seated across the room. He had no hair and very little meat on his bones. Fritz had observed his hand tremble when he raised his fork. "Just for your information, I'll tell you this. That man has syphilis. Probably caught it on a riverboat or in some betting parlor. He has no one to call family. He no longer gambles but lives on the boat, waiting to die from one of the diseases inappropriate sex can transfer. If you haven't already found out, the madams on the boat are as powerful and rich as most gamblers—each has her bevy of soiled doves." Franz faintly smiled and lowered his chin as he lifted his eyebrows to detect if Fritz caught his drift.

"It's work time, my boy. Let's go get them. Do you have your purse?"

"No."

"Well, let's go get it. How are you going to gamble without clinking stuff?"

They went to the safe, picked up his bag, and then headed toward Fritz's room. There was a noticeable absence of the usual tourist gamblers. When they walked into his room, it was packed with high rollers who gave applause to Fritz. At his table sat a man in tailored attire, large diamond rings and stick pin, the perfect archetype of the dangerous game's professional. "Son of a gun," exclaimed Franz, "if it isn't Rattlesnake Jack. The last time I saw you, a black leg was chasing you." A roar of laughter rose to the joke—if it was a joke.

"Fritz, you've just been challenged by the most infamous gambler on the circuit. There are few men, if any, in this room who would give him a chance to cheat them. I suspect"—Franz glanced around the room—"that someone hopped off the boat when we stopped in Vicksburg and recruited Rattlesnake to challenge you." Again his eyes scanned the crowd, hoping to detect a suspect.

Hearing and seeing the occasion, Fritz developed an itch he was hankering to scratch.

"Gentlemen"—he smiled and spread his arms toward the table—"it appears we have a game to play. We can seat five. Feel free to join in." No one moved. The atmosphere was more that of a funeral parlor than a bluff game.

The time was five minutes past nine in the evening. Fritz took a new deck, with the usual card numbers two through six removed, the rule for five-card draw. He made a perfunctory shuffle, split the deck, and rolled his open hand to Rattlesnake Jack, who did the same.

Rattlesnake won the cut and dealt five cards to each. Fritz, as fast as swatting a fly, picked up his cards and laid a wager rarely seen, five twenty-dollar gold pieces on the table. Rattlesnake covered, discarded two cards, and drew. He studied his hand and raised a twenty-dollar eagle. Fritz was pecking his forefinger on the table as if impatient, and before Rattlesnake's coin settled, he covered it and raised the bet with five more twenty-dollar gleamers, a pot most gamblers had never heard of.

The crowd was mute. Gamblers in the rear of the room were on tiptoes, some on anything they could stand on. Waiting. Breathless.

Fritz cocked his head and smiled. "I'll take one card, please." He had the card in hand before Rattlesnake had pulled his hand back. A quick look. He reached for his purse, took out forty more gold dollars, and counted them one by one onto the existing pot.

Rattlesnake's face looked like a dead man's. He could only stare. Finally, he said, "I'm out."

As Rattlesnake left the room unwilling to speak, Fritz was raking his bright twenty-dollar gold coins into his purse. No one ever knew the hand Fritz held. A sly grin from Franz indicated his suspicion.

Before the Snake closed the door, Fritz called, "Thank you for the game, sir."

CHAPTER 10

Fritz awoke to a buzz of activity. The ship hands were busy and passengers excited. New Orleans sprawled across the skyline. Negroes and coon asses alike scrambled to unload and reload freightage. Dozens of barefooted women peddled baubles or fruit, and scantily clad children begged with outstretched open hands. From the balconies of French architecture, ravishing, raven-haired beauties of French, Negro, Indian, and Cajun interbreeds advertised their debauchery in exchange for the immoral golden handshake.

Fritz had never heard of nor dreamed there was such a place. His overnight layover on Bourbon Street was a time never to be forgotten or explained. After twenty-four hours of sightseeing and no sleep, the steamboat was reboarded and began crawling against the current northward.

After a long sleep, he emerged from his room and began strolling about. Half of those aboard were new passengers from Cajun land.

Like all young men, he awoke hungry and soon found himself in the dining area. It was alive and humming with excited travelers. When he sat, he froze. *That face, it can't be. That man went over the cliff. Brisco is dead!*

The man's eyes were likewise fixed on Fritz. The man rose, left the room, leaving Fritz lost in his confusion. *Have I seen a ghost? That had to be Brisco. It couldn't be Brisco. Brisco tried to kill me, but then he died. I know he died. I saw him die! Am I losing my sanity?*

He ordered a whiskey, the first drop of alcohol ever to touch his lips. He took one swig, coughed, and then rose and walked out of the crowded room, looking left and right as he exited the door. He went directly to his room. There would be no gambling tonight. His mind was too jumbled.

Come midnight, sleep had eluded him. Tired of fidgeting and pacing, he decided to look up Franz. Perhaps watching him wield his magic in a game would calm him. His room overlooked the deck, with its outside railing eight feet away. He stepped out, walked to a corner, and turned.

There, face-to-face, stood that man. "Brisco?"

"No, damn you, I'm Rosco, Brisco Earley's twin brother, and I'm here to send you to hell to be with him. I saw you in Best while you were being arrested. I was at the trial when you were convicted to hang. At the hanging, I knew something was fishy when that uncle of yours hauled you out from behind that fence. I, like everyone else, thought you were dead until today. Well, now I get the privilege to cut your heart out and feed it to the catfish."

Fritz had never been a fighter. He was always a peace lover and peace maker. He had no fighting skills. He never needed them. Now he faced a man, wild with revenge and rage. Rosco jerked from his pocket a switchblade knife with a six-inch blade reflecting off the dim oil lamps of the ship's walkway. He lunged forward. Fritz, with no knowledge of defense, stepped to his left and kicked Rosco in the groin. He bellowed and doubled over, yelling expletives and curses that would embarrass a demon. Fritz tried to run, but Rosco managed to trip him. He leaped on top of Fritz's body. Lifting the knife in his right hand, he growled, "I'll slit your throat, you bastard."

Fritz was able to catch the wrist that held the weapon. Then he remembered, *only for life or death*. He triggered the release, which he had practiced again and again, and the .41-caliber derringer fell into his right palm. He cocked and shot the first bullet upward from just below the rib cage. Rosco was startled. His countenance showed horror.

"You son of—" Fritz stopped his sentence with the second bullet someplace in his mid to upper body. Rosco lost his strength and rolled off Fritz's body.

The .41 Remington derringer, an over and under with three-inch barrels, was not a deadly weapon; the large diameter bullet was propelled by a relatively small measure of powder. It was actually known to be an escape gun, manufactured for and carried mostly by gamblers and prostitutes, giving an edge to escape. That night it did exactly what Sunday planned when he packed it for him. It saved his life.

He did the first thing that popped into his mind. He grabbed Rosco by the ankles and slid him overboard. He grabbed buckets of water, standing by in case of fire, and washed the blood from the deck. He ran, partially stumbling, to his room and collapsed on his bed. His nerves were shattered, his mind spinning in every direction. *Was the man dead when I pushed him overboard? Might he resurface like Franz did? Will this matter of Brisco and Rosco follow me to my grave? Oh, my God,* he prayed, *I trust you to hold me close to yourself in this matter—in Jesus's name, I pray.*

Before dawn, Franz came hunting him, having not seen him during the night. Entering the room, he knew something drastic had happened.

"Fritz, sit up." Franz lifted his head from the bed and placed a wet towel over his brow. "Tell me, boy, what happened? Speak to me, Fritz."

"I killed him, Franz. I killed the twin brother of the man who fell on my ax in North Carolina, the man I was convicted to hang for murdering."

Fritz was speaking incoherently, his breathing labored. "He said his name was Rosco Earley, that he recognized me from my trial."

"Rosco Earley. Brisco. I knew those brothers, two of the most debased crooks ever to ride the riverboats. They picked pockets, working together to divert their victim's attention. They weren't gamblers. They were con artists, sleight-of-hand magicians, kings of deception. They were permanently banned from the river, could not enter any of the steamships." Franz slowly lifted his head in thought; his eyes closed. He pushed, as if he was trying to catch his breath, but then said, "The last I heard of them, they were working the mountains, robbing lone travelers, even killing some of their victims. If they are who you say they are, you have done humanity a great favor."

"Yes, but just think of all the grief they caused me and the price I'm paying."

"Wait, my boy, to receive suffering from an adversary is one thing, but overcoming adversity is another." Franz had become somber, digging deep down in his thoughts.

"I have been thinking seriously about your conversation about your God and how he has led and protected you." He waited, scratched his thin gray hair, and continued, "I've followed your life as you've retold it—one miracle after another. You have been vindicated, at least against these two who have tried to kill you. If there is a hell, surely those two are there. It is not my place to judge, but that is how I feel."

Fritz was deep in thought. He said not a word.

Franz started to speak, but Fritz interrupted him. "If I had the one miracle, it would be the woman I carry in my heart, Willa. If I had her by my side, I could face anything." His loneliness seemed unbearable living each day in the company of memories.

"Well, Fritz, tell you what I'll do. I'll try to pitch in a little faith and help you. Let's make it a project. I'm going to see what kind of God you have. Deal?" The two made a friendly handshake.

"Deal." Fritz smiled for the first time in days. A glimmer of hope shined in his mind that just maybe there would be a time when he might see the love of his life again.

Vicksburg was the next stop to load and unload freightage and passengers. At dockside, Franz collapsed. The ship's assistants placed him in a carriage and hauled him to a hospital. The doctors, well trained since most of them had practiced through the bloody war years, examined him.

Their prognosis was not good. "This man has an extremely weak heart. He must maintain a strict diet regime, some assistance walking, and relieved of all stress possible." They prescribed medicine and sent a letter to his doctor in Memphis.

Fortunately, mechanical problems delayed the steamboat's departure for two days. This gave Franz some convalescent time. He was allowed to ride a carriage back to the boat. The next stop, home.

Fritz and Franz had made a scandalous amount of gold. They had also won a nice stack of U.S. certificates. These were valuable, but they also left a paper trail. Gamblers avoided them as much as possible. The big problem of making and hording large sums of cash was spending it. That being the case, many said, what good was it if you couldn't spend it? Most gamblers didn't face that problem. If they stayed at the game long enough, it eventually disappeared. A common saying among them was, "Gambling money has no home."

That subject was discussed often among the gambling fraternity. Some believed it to be an addiction or some kind of disease, the same as alcohol or tobacco or other drugs. Once a person got hooked, very few ever stopped, regardless of their losses or circumstances.

Franz, always the deep thinker—some said a philosopher, once told Fritz, "Perhaps a day will come in the future when doctors will discover a way to treat such problems, alongside other nonphysical diseases."

The *Robert E. Lee* paddled north, finally docking in Memphis.

Fritz took complete charge now, insisting that Franz rest. He hired help with their luggage and the trunk, now heavy-laden, primarily with gold. He sent for the funeral carriage for Franz to travel in, immediately taking him to the office of his personal physician. The doctor would not allow them to leave, but stay overnight for further diagnosis.

The results: bad. It was determined that Franz indeed had a bad heart, but the worst discovery was he had tuberculosis, a disease the medical field knew very little about. "Of this we are certain," the doctor said, "the Mississippi River area is no place for a person with this disease. It appears the tuberculosis has affected his heart and, even worse, his lungs." The doctor spoke gravely. "I recommend a complete change of environment, high altitude—the higher above sea level the better. The Rockies would be good, but there are few good doctors on that frontier. Maybe"—he pondered a moment—"the Appalachians or Alleghenies. I will research an area where you can be under the care of the appropriate doctors—if there is such a place." The doctor seemed to be combing his mind for recommendations.

"Mr. Buckner, you come back in two days. I will research and compound some medicine for Mr. Beuchner's illness."

And so they departed, gently conveying him to his mansion, lying in a funeral carriage for comfort.

Fritz took over all the affairs of Franz, the employees and his businesses, which he learned were monumental.

On the second day, Franz was not up to travel. Fritz made the trip to get his medicine. Before departure, Franz called him to his room. "Hand this letter to my lawyer. Wait and bring back his answer to me." In another envelope was a large sum of money.

Fritz did not know the letter contents, but he knew it was important. He handled the matters expeditiously and then eagerly returned home.

On his arrival, the estate was in pandemonium, and Mutt was lunging on his chain, barking frantically.

"Two men pushed their way past us and kidnapped Mr. Beuchner. There was nothing we could do. They bound his hands and ran, partially dragging him. You know how weak he was." Everyone was hysterical.

"Were they on horseback? Buggy?"

"None of us saw any such. They disappeared on foot. They vanished into those woods yonder."

Fritz realized exactly where they were headed and was reasonably certain whom they were, black legs hired by the man who thought he had killed Franz and threw him into the river. They were headed west, down the trail that went directly to an overhanging cliff above Chickasaw Bluff.

Moving swiftly, he first touched the inside of his right wrist. He could feel the cold steel of the derringer against his fingertips. He ran to the chain that secured Mutt, loosened it from its hold, and put him on the scent trail of the kidnappers. He had difficulty holding on to the chain as the huge dog pulled him along the woodland path.

God, give me time. Let me reach them before they kill him.

Thankfully, Mutt was a silent trailer. He didn't bark as he pursued, thus the black legs, if so they were, had no idea they were being chased. They were within twenty paces of the cliff when Fritz and Mutt broke out of the bush. He loosed the almost one hundred pounds of canine fury, and within three leaps he had one of the murderers by the throat. Mutt crashed into his victim, bringing them both precariously close the edge of the cliff. Immediately, Fritz was on the back of the other. The man tried to pull out a revolver in an attempt to even the odds, but Fritz knocked it away, and it tumbled over the edge of the cliff. Mutt was in control of his victim who was frantically trying to extricate himself while Fritz was simply trying to just hold on. The man frantically tried punching behind him, attempting to land a blow on Fritz. Franz was free but was on the ground in exhaustion. Fritz's man was spinning, trying to shake him loose. During the struggle, they were inching closer to the cliff edge, so close that Fritz feared that both of them might go over. He timed the spin, and as he passed the safe side, he turned loose. That threw the man off balance, and before he could regain control, he went over, and in doing so, he bumped his cohort with Mutt clamped to his throat. All three went over the precipice. Fritz screamed, "Mutt!" Unnerved and trembling, Fritz crawled to the edge and looked down. The merciless Mississippi had created a swirl in rounding the humongous rock, and they were all hopelessly caught in the vortex. They perished with Mutt still locked on the man's neck.

Now, all of Fritz's attention turned to Franz, weak but alert.

"I'm fine, boy, thanks to you. That's twice you've saved me from that river. I can never repay you."

"Who do you suppose those men were? Why did they try to kill you?"

"Likely they were hired by Lyndon James, the gambler who tried to kill me when you saved me the first time. He is bitter. He may try again. When you win all of a man's money and take his woman, some men become insatiably vindictive. Revenge becomes their only purpose in life."

He tried to carry Franz, but the pain throughout his body forbade it. Fritz broke strong dead limbs and made a toboggan, lacing it together with his and Franz's leather shoe strings and strips torn from his shirt—a device he had learned to build from the Cherokees.

The pair broke out of the woods to the shouting voices of happiness.

When life calmed somewhat, he reported to Franz that his attorney would be there at nine o'clock in the morning.

Fritz took a long walk alone, grieving the loss of his faithful dog.

At nine o'clock, Franz's lawyer rolled into Franz's cart way. A groom attended to his horse while Fritz led him to Franz's lounge chair, which had piles of folders beside him on a table.

After their initial greeting and a pot of coffee was put in place, Franz came straight to the point. "Most of my sunsets are behind me, and the doctor has confirmed my belief that I am not long for this world. I have no living relative that I'm aware of. I'm authorizing you to draft my will and leave everything I own to this young man to whom I owe my life, twice over. He has proven faithful to me and stood beside me in my times of life-and-death crises." The lawyer took rapid notes, seeking to capture not only Franz's words but his intent.

"You know the extent of my holdings, having been my agent over the years. I want you to sell everything I own and deposit it in Fritz Buckner's account. Everything." Franz's eyes never left the solemn face of his attorney.

"I am confident Fritz will care for me until I leave this world. I have no apprehension of leaving myself in his hands." Allowing a few moments for the attorney to organize his thoughts, Franz asked, "Do you have any questions?"

"None of any consequence just now. I feel I have a handle on your wishes."

"Another thing. I'm sure you are aware I have a considerable amount of cash, mostly in the form of gold coinage. All that is to go to Fritz. Arrange for the U.S. certificates I own to be legally transferred to Fritz."

"We can arrange that, Franz."

"When this estate sells, give my employees who have been loyal to me—all of them—over the years a one-year salary as a severance gift. This will tide them over until they can reestablish their lives.

"So you are my attorney, my sales agent, and whatever else it takes to put my end of life in order. I want everything to be bound legally so that nothing can be challenged by anyone. Now, any questions?"

"Not at this time."

"Fritz, do you have any discussion about any of these matters?"

"No, sir."

"One more item," Franz interjected, "whatever your legal fee, above your expenses, add twenty-five percent as a gratuity from me for all your years of faithful service."

"Thank you, Franz. I shall have this commission completed expeditiously."

"One final matter. There are three men, all gamblers, whom I've known over the years. I call them friends. Each has asked me if I ever chose to sell my estate, they wanted an opportunity to buy it. The fourth man, I will give you his name, is a man who will be able to contact them since they stay on the move most of the time. They have the cash. Take payment in gold. Take measures to get it to Fritz." Franz paused to reflect.

"These other two names I am giving you are men who can knowledgeably appraise my estate. Hire them to each submit an appraisal and use that as a negotiating tool. With everything considered, I leave it with you. Sell to the highest bidder. Above all, cheat no one.

"Make certain all taxes are paid. I'm trusting you to make the transfers clean and that Fritz will encounter no problems when I'm gone. Of greatest importance, protect Fritz.

"Now, if you gentlemen will excuse me, I need a nap."

Except for necessities, Fritz sat near Franz's door, ready to respond to any need. All the employees from the household, to the stables, and to the fields loved Franz. Each did his or her best to make him comfortable.

The will, all the legal work, and appraisals were handled with promptness. The three buyers were in a bidding contest, being refereed by the lawyer. Each wanted it badly, but they were both on friendly terms. The successful bidder had the cash, in gold. When he handed it over, the weight was considerable.

As if Fritz didn't have enough to occupy him, he realized his unfulfilled life without the one he loved was worse than a lifetime in prison or death. His mind was set. Some way he must have Willa, but how?

The repairs to the bridge crossing the Mississippi River were now complete. Hundreds were crossing over it every day, most going with practically nothing to begin a new life. Fritz now realized he could go to Texas, blend into the frontier life, buy a ranch, or even go to California and purchase a producing gold mine. His fortune could be invested and give him a life of extravagance, just using the interest. He could buy an entire town, but for what purpose? Willa was his life, the center of his universe.

On a sunny day, Fritz helped Franz to the seats under the giant shade tree. A large pitcher of tea sat before them, and the two men, each loving and trusting the other, released their thoughts after a long reflection.

"Franz, last night I recollected something Uncle Sunday told me. Since the war, things were changing dramatically back home. The railroad is coming, he said. He swore that a man's voice will travel across the wire lines within ten years. Those things stagger my mind, but most of his predictions have come to pass.

"Lying in my bed, something came to my mind that I had completely forgotten. Uncle Sunday told me that plans were in the making to build a tuberculosis research hospital in Black Mountain. Franz, that's less than ten miles from where Brisco fell on my ax and killed himself." Franz leaned forward as if trying to comprehend the direction Fritz was going with his abstract thinking.

"Then my memory jumped track, and I remembered what your doctor told you. 'Leave this Mississippi environment. Altitude,' he said, 'the Appalachians, and appropriate doctors.'" Fritz was excited, his eyes beaming, "Oh yes, and Uncle Sunday said as far as he knew it was the first such hospital in the United States."

"And so?" queried Franz.

"And so, I'll take you back there where you can get the best treatment in the country. You can visit with Uncle Sunday. He is hungry for like-minded friendship."

"Yes, and they'll hang you for good. Are you brain cracked, my boy? You can't go back there, ever."

"Well, I've been pondering that one too. I have decided to go back there in secrecy and get Willa. A life without Willa is worse than death. I must do it." His chin quivered, and his eyes teared, but he managed to continue. "I love and respect you, Franz. You have given me everything you own, but I remember reading in a book of Uncle Sunday's, a man is not free until he owns possessions, and then he is not free because they own him. For me, life is not worth living without Willa. My homesickness for her seems unbearable at times. I live each day walking with her in my heart. My unquenchable desire for her takes me by the throat."

Franz had said nothing; his wisdom allowed Fritz to unburden his soul. After a pause, he reached out and touched him. "I never took time to fall in love and marry. Many times I've regretted it." He blinked. "If that is your true heart speaking, I think you should go for it. You are a gambler, remember?"

Fritz leaped and yelled, "Yes!"

Employees who were in sight stopped to look at the ecstatic young man jumping for joy.

CHAPTER 11

"Vote for Sunday Boys, Sheriff of Buncombe County." Sunday had formally announced his candidacy for sheriff.

Western North Carolina was one of the hardest hit areas of the Civil War, not in military casualties but because its allegiance was so divided. Approximately one-half of the people wanted to remain loyal to the Union. The United States had been freed from the English crown by the blood of their ancestors. The war to these people was not against slavery. Many in the mountains didn't know what slavery was, and most had never even seen a Negro.

The other half wanted to be loyal to the state of North Carolina whose politicians had voted to join other southern states and seceded from the Union of the United States of America.

Both the Union and Confederacy recruited among the two mountain factions, and if a family of either side refused, lives and homes were destroyed. The mountain people were devastated.

Sunday Boys was a native of Buncombe County, North Carolina, who by circumstances was absent during the conflict. Now home, he was determined to help rebuild the county of his boyhood.

Being one of only a few natives with an education, his campaign speeches cut straight to the quick. "We must establish law and order," the six-foot-four, two-hundred-sixty-five-pound man thundered. "Buncombe County must have a sheriff who himself obeys the law and who cannot be bought off by the crooks themselves."

The line was clearly drawn. Everyone knew Sunday had the unlawful trial of his nephew in his memory, and many suspected that to be part of his motive to run for sheriff.

"We have no railroad here, even though the rest of the state has it. We must have bridges. We have no all-weather roads in spite of the fact we are the crossroads of commerce from Tennessee, South Carolina, and Virginia. I want to be part of an administration that brings progress." This was the platform of Sunday Boys.

Zackary Pearson campaigned like a desperate man, doing everything he could to hold the office that kept his pockets full of hush money, and his crooked friends were influencing their friends with liquor, wanton women, or anything that would swing their votes.

Sunday ran a campaign clean as a hound's tooth—no mudslinging, simply an appeal for law and order and the economic good for all the people. The consensus was that he was winning enough support to win the election.

It appeared Zackary had run low on powder for his campaign gun until a man walked into the sheriff's office. "My name is Rosco Early," the man announced.

"I am the twin brother of the man who was murdered by Sky Boys. I attended the trial and sat ten feet from him. I studied every feature of the murderer."

Sheriff Zack Pearson could not believe what he was hearing. He assumed that the trial and hanging was well in the past and forgotten, just like dozens of his other rigged trials he had set up.

"He's not dead. I swear it on my brother's grave. He is alive and well, gambling on the *Robert E. Lee* riverboat on the Mississippi River. When I recognized him, I tried to kill him in revenge for murdering my brother, but the little devil shot me twice and threw me in the river. I'm sure he thought I was dead, and I damn near was."

Zack sat, unable to comprehend what he was hearing.

"I managed to swim ashore, and some man picked me up and took me to a doctor, and I managed to survive. I wanted to kill him, and I'd still like to open his guts, but two bullets is enough. I decided my best revenge was to report to you where he is and let you take care of him."

"Are you touched in the head, man? We hung Sky Boys. He's dead and buried."

"Were you at the hanging, Sheriff?"

"No, but many of my friends were. I've seen his grave."

"Sheriff, I was at the hanging. I saw it. That uncle of his hoodwinked everybody. That fence around the gallows hid the actual hanging. When Sunday Boys drove his wagon out of that fence, he was like a man escaping from hell. He and his gang disappeared before anybody could figure out what happened."

Zack was incredulous.

"I tell you, Sheriff, Sky Boys is alive."

"You sign an affidavit for what you just told me, and I'll see to it you get your revenge. I'll let you trip the trigger to the trap door he falls through at his hanging."

Smiling, Rosco said, "Get it ready. I'll sign it."

Thoughts that the sheriff had stuffed away began to surface, like many of his crooked shenanigans. The story of the Haywood County sheriff and the two town drunks who said they had seen Sky get out of his casket and run refreshed his memory.

Within two hours, Sheriff Zack was pounding leather heading west to Waynesville.

"Is 'at so, Zack? I told ye. You jest didn't believe me."

"Can you round up those two men so I can question them?"

"Well, I might, but, Zack, I ain't been paid fer the things I done fer ye in the past. How's about some frog skins fer the favors you're a axing?"

"Listen, man, this is no time to be haggling with the law. You help me in this, and I'll see you get your money."

Sheriff Creed Gamble spat a stream of tobacco juice, wiped his chin, and looked at Zack.

"Oh hell, Creed, I got five dollar on me. That's all I got. Here, take it, and let's roust those men up."

It didn't take long to find the inebriates drowning worms in Raccoon Creek.

"Well now, Sheriff, we gone to lots a trouble to help ye. How's about a jug of shine to bring back our reklecsion?"

"C'mon, fellers. I got some rotgut in my office. Let's get Zack here back on the road."

Zack had affidavits in his pocket. The boozers made their Xs. Creed made his mark and got someone who was walking along the road to witness his X, and Zack struck out for his Buncombe County office.

With the affidavits in hand, Sheriff Zack obtained a court order to dig up the grave in front of the marker of Sky Boys.

Two men, six hours, down six feet, they thumped the casket lid. Of course, the sheriff had his witnesses standing by.

"Well, open the thing." The men, holding rags over their noses and mouths unlatched and opened the lid. Inside, they found a log. "So that's all they buried? That conniving bastard Sunday Boys! I'll can his ass for this! He's just reelected me for sheriff." With more signed affidavits, Sheriff Zackary Pearson went directly to the home of Sunday Boys.

Standing in the yard of Sunday's home, Zack fired repeated gunshots into the air to draw a crowd. With great hullabaloo, he called for Sunday to come outside. "I'm arrestin' you, Sunday Boys, for assisting the escape of a convicted murderer. Put out your hands." He snapped a set of heavy leg irons on the wrists of Sunday.

With all the fanfare he could muster, he led Sunday Boys back along the muddy road from Best to Asheville and then up and down the town's dirt streets for a show-off; politics not excepted.

The following day, Zack had all the Elect Sunday Boys signs covered with a reward poster: "One thousand dollars reward for the capture of Sky Boys. Dead or alive."

The county was in turmoil.

CHAPTER 12

Fritz and Franz solidified their plans. The pair would leave Memphis together. Fritz would return to western North Carolina, secretly pick up Willa, and they would leave together. Fritz decided he and Willa would take a more southerly route to Texas, having learned the railroads were tying in to the major cities. They would rough it to South Carolina and then ride the trains from there on. He now had accessible money to begin life anew without financial hardship. He was always aware that secrecy must always be forefront.

Franz, with no family ties and no close friends, easily chose to relocate in the Asheville area where the altitude was nearly one-half mile above sea level and had a tuberculosis research center in the making, if not already completed.

Franz was the master planner, but Fritz insisted on a slow pace and much rest for his friend. He nit-picked the legal work to make certain Fritz would encounter no problems with the estate settlement and his inheritance.

Because of the huge amount of money involved and the shaky post-war economy, the attorney suggested they set up accounts in four different banks.

After the accounts were set up and monies deposited, Franz suggested that Fritz make withdrawals from each. "A trial run," as Franz called it.

Lo and behold, there was a glitch at every bank, the proof of who he was. That proved to be no small problem.

"I can arrange that, Franz, but it will involve a lot of time and money."

"Have I ever haggled with you about money?" He was insulted at the suggestion.

"Forgive me, please. I did err in my statement. Of course you haven't. I shall give my undivided attention to this matter."

"That's what I like to hear." Franz, the man who paid the bill, smiled.

In this matter, the destruction left by the war was a bit helpful. The attorney hired two assistants and put them on the project. They were unaware of the purpose of their research.

First, they sought out families by the name of Buckner. From among those, they located people whose family units had been killed in their entirety. Next, the task was to find a family Bible with a family history and genealogical page that was not filled in completely. When the lawyer and his associates finished their finagling, he finalized his work by legally recording it.

The attorney earned his fee by methodically giving Fritz a family and a birthday.

"Fritz, this Bible contains your life," the lawyer advised with solemnity. "Guard it as such. Take this and withdraw your money." That he did, and he switched his money back and forth among the banks.

"Fritz, I know you are an honest person, but let this be a lesson," Franz admonished. "With enough money, you can accomplish almost anything."

"In this case, I'm glad that was true. However, I still want my life to be built on integrity. I want my word to be my bond. Thanks for the advice, anyway."

"If you are going back to your old haunts, you need to change your appearance. Let your beard grow. Change the way you brush your hair completely. Change the style clothes you wore back then." Franz scratched his head. "Oh yes, remember to do nothing the way you once did. Whew"—Franz chuckled—"you're sure going to be walking a tight rope, my boy. Luck to you."

The two men shopped together and bought appropriate wardrobes for Fritz, business attire for their train travel to Chattanooga, and ordinary clothes for the carriage ride through the Smoky Mountains.

Franz commissioned a journeyman carriage craftsman.

"I have urgent business," he explained. "I will pay you twice your normal charge to design and build a special carriage. I am not well. The doctor tells me I must recline for much of my time when I travel. I'll need a comfortable bed built into the unit. Of utmost importance, I need a specially designed floor."

Franz leaned toward the builder and spoke softly as if in secrecy. "I'll need to roll flat some large maps and designs and to protect them from foul weather. This is highly secret work for the government. You must keep this confidential. I'm sure you understand. Can you build for me a false double floor to meet these standards?"

"I can do that, sir. Are there other requirements?"

"Only one other. I want you to age the carriage. Make it appear to have seen hard use. Of course, we'll need a couple of spare wheels mounted underneath, cotters, tools, and ample grease."

"That I can do. How soon do you need this?"

"Sparing no expense, of course, as soon as possible."

Franz, giving his most serious look, spoke softly. "You know how it is… The government wants it yesterday."

"I need two full weeks, three at the most. The parts I do not have I will make. Will you leave a deposit?"

"A deposit, my good man? I shall give you gold now for your normal charges and the balance in cold cash when I return in twenty-one days."

While Franz was handling the mechanical matter, Fritz was at the gunsmith. "I want the latest model repeating rifle."

"That would be a lever-action Henry, of course. The Union soldiers who were lucky enough to get one said they could load it on Sunday and shoot it all week." The gunsmith laughed as if he had told an original story. "Anyway, I have one. They are hard to find, you know. It's a .44 caliber, shoots fifteen shots without reload. The twenty-four-inch barrel makes it an easy handler."

With no more said, Fritz pulled from his pocket a fold of several bills.

"I'll take it, and four boxes of cartridges. Does it come in a box? I'm not comfortable carrying a rifle around town."

"I have the original box, yes, but everybody else carries a gun. You need not fret about that."

"I'm not a gunfighter or a hunter, but I have property, and someday I may need a rifle. You know, maybe to shoot a prairie dog or coyote."

Three horses were chosen with care, ones with superior training under harness and superb stamina for the long trip. The third would walk behind to give each a rest at intervals. They bought used but good harness and rigging. In choosing, they wanted an ordinary look, not fancy, which could possibly arouse questions. Their intentions were to appear as any other traveler of the day. All their supplies were laid out in readiness. They obtained buckets for water and feed and had extra shoes fitted for each horse. This assignment fit well into Fritz's former freighting experience.

They led their horses to take delivery of the custom-made carriage. A double check proved the maker to be as recommended, an expert. "You well earned your double pay." Franz enjoyed the delight on the man's face as he handed over the agreed double price in folding money.

The final step revealed a sight few people ever see: more gold in coins than a man could lift. It was the accumulation of a lifetime, the winnings stashed away by a professional gambler. Not his wealth in property and investments but brilliant, naked, gold coins, each in the larger denominations. It was more wealth than a dozen men could spend in a life span living luxuriously.

Fritz gasped. "Where in heaven's name are we going to put all this gold?" This was one of the rare occasions Franz gave a genuine belly laugh.

"That matter has been arranged. Give me a hand." Grasping two carefully concealed handle rings, they lifted the meticulously fitted lid covering the false bottom in the carriage floor. Instead of "highly secret" government maps and designs, Fritz lifted, one by one, five containers of highly secret United States issued gold coins. They spread them out across the bottom floor and then padded them with thick quilting and replaced the lid.

Franz handled the travel arrangements for the train to Nashville, then to Chattanooga, one Pullman seat for himself and an empty freight car for the carriage and Fritz. He would remain with the horses, insuring their calmness and safety.

They rented a hotel room on the eastern side of Memphis, paying in advance. Their travel needs demanded only their necessities, enabling them to transfer the items with ease from the mansion to hotel.

Every item had been checked repeatedly; no stone was left unturned. After midnight on the twenty-first day, the horses were rigged, hitched to the carriage, and everything loaded. By prior arrangement, a ramp was in place beside the train car for the carriage and horses to load. It was all expedited in minutes, and the train pulled away with Franz and Fritz departing in total secrecy.

Ike Godfrey had been fired from the Pinkerton Detective Agency, a good man but too aggressive, or so they said. Ike made his expertise available for hire, and he was contracted by a gambler named Lyndon James.

"I will pay all your expenses and ten percent above your Pinkerton salary. The man I want you to locate is Franz Beuchner. I've had an amateur watching his movements in Memphis, but he slipped away without a trace. No one is able to determine the direction he headed. He's a sly one." Lyndon squinted his eyes. "He and a young man who hangs with him evidently killed two black legs I put on him."

"Wait, hold it right there," Ike interjected. "I'll take no job where a killing is involved. I'm out."

"Hold on. Don't go jumping out of the trace-chains. You'll not be involved in any killing. All I want is to have the man located. I'll pay you one half in cash now and the balance when you find him. Send me a telegram, and I'll race to you on the next train. You keep a trace on him. I'll come to you. When my opportunity comes, you'll be handed your money, and you can be gone. Can we agree on that?"

"I'll do it, but you remember one thing. I have my weapon, and I'll use it on you if you double cross me or break your word," Ike spoke with an immobilizing stare. "That man you call Franz means nothing to me, nor do you. Only a payday."

With that, Lyndon gave him a hefty advance. Ike hopped on the cold trail like a hunting hound.

Here, there, and about. To the hotels. Oh yes, two men. Secrecy. Gone in the morning's wee hours. Then the trail froze. A train ticket. Only one? Oh yes, a carriage, horses, and an attendant in an empty boxcar. Now why the—? Oh yes.

The telegraph was short and simple: "Leave at daybreak on train to Nashville."

When Lyndon stepped off the train, he was carrying a leather bootlike case, obviously containing a rifle.

"We're running behind," Ike barked. "Run over there and buy tickets on the next train to Chattanooga. God only knows where they'll head next. They're pulling a carriage, which they'll launch somewhere, to someplace. Wherever it is they are heading has no rail line. I can assure you of that. That doesn't help much, but we've got at least a sniff to follow."

They were forty-eight hours behind Fritz and Franz when they disembarked in Chattanooga. "Yep, I know which way the wagon went," said a luggage handler, with an outstretched hand and an expectant expression. With the drop of a twenty-cent piece, the hand didn't move, only a slight twitch of the fingers. A trade dollar lubricated the man's lips. "They went yonder way." He pointed east.

"Uh huh, I would have won that bet," Ike spoke and hummed a tune to himself as he thought. "Those two are headed straight for the Great Smoky Mountains." He hummed some more. "I'll wager my trigger finger they're headed to the vicinity of Asheville, North Carolina. If not there, then not too far away. There's no rail line to Asheville.

"Let's get some horses. We'll try to make up time and catch them in the wilderness before they reach civilization on the other side."

No one would rent them a horse. Lyndon dug down into his cash and bought two decent-looking horses along with the gear for riding. One saddle had a rifle boot.

Fortunately for them, there were few travelers heading into the foothills, and Ike was able to make out carriage tracks.

"Get off that horse, Lyndon, and look here." He measured with his hands the width of the wheels. "This outfit is four inches wider than a standard carriage wheel-spread." Looking at Lyndon, he said, "That carriage for some reason was special made. The rig is heavy too. Look how deep the wheel tracks are. Umm, better think on that one. Let's move along. We're gaining slowly."

Fritz and Franz moved along without hurry. Franz was fascinated with the mountain beauty and the never-ending haze that enshrouded the mountains, giving the Smokies its name.

"Fritz, I've been thinking seriously about your life, your faith in God and Jesus Christ. Having seen how the Almighty has cared for you through all the trials you've had to face, overcoming them all, I'm convinced there is something to this faith thing." Franz paused. Fritz listened. "Is it possible that I could, in some way, connect with your God?" His question was asked sincerely with deep intensity.

"Franz, I don't know how to answer your question. All I can do is tell you my own experience. I've been to a few religious meetings, but what I heard there has no relationship to what I have inside me." Fritz was reaching deep within himself for words.

"Uncle Sunday helped me a lot because he has studied God's Word, the Bible. He explained to me that our Creator loves us in spite of our sins and failures. He said, and he read it to me out of the Bible, that Jesus Christ was God's Son who came into this world and died on a cross for everyone who would trust him. Uncle Sunday said that while his Son, Jesus, was on the cross, God placed the guilt of our sins on him and that Jesus died for us. Uncle Sunday said if I'd ask God in faith to forgive my sins, he would enter my life. He said that his presence would guide me and give me the peace. He said, when I die God would bring me to heaven to be with him forever." Fritz was praying inside himself and talking to Franz at the same time. *God, help me to say the right thing. Give Franz an understanding of your love. Draw him by your grace.*

"Franz, I don't understand it all. Uncle Sunday said I didn't have to but to just trust God. Well, in short, I did that, and from that moment I have been able to sense God's presence in my life. I talk to God every day, just like I talk to you. Even in my troubles, I have peace."

The carriage bumped and rumbled over the mountain roads, which became worse with every mile.

"If I didn't answer your question, forgive me. That's all I know. I truly wish you could feel the presence of God and find that inner peace that he has given me."

"Thank you, my boy. I'm going to think on that. Right now I'm going to lie down in the carriage.

Perhaps you can pray for me to have the understanding and the faith."

"I'll swap the horses out while you move to your bed. Now's a good time to water the horses in that branch over there while we have stopped."

They reached Cleveland and stopped for the night at a small rooming house for travelers to rest before embarking into the Smokies. Fritz bought grain for the horses and a supply for three more days on the road. He rented stable space for the night and gave the animals a rubdown before giving attention to himself. The rooming house meal was sparse but adequate.

"Whoa, whoa. We're up with them." Ike lifted his hand. "See that carriage yonder? That's it. We'd better back off and give them time in the morning to move out," Ike advised.

"I'm going to ride with you two more days. I'm convinced those two are headed to Asheville. The road will split in Murphy, just over the North Carolina line. They will have to take one of the two. The southern route will follow the Ocoee River gorge and go through the Balsam Mountains. The other road goes through the Cherokee country and Soco Gap at the crest of the Smokies. I'll predict the latter."

Ike was emphatic. "Pay me up now. I've led you to them. Give me two additional days' pay, and I'll go along to the road split in Murphy."

Lyndon counted out the Pinkerton's payment, and they slept on a bed of forest leaves that night.

During the next two days, Fritz sensed he was in the presence of a new man. Franz was relaxed, smiled, and seemed at peace with himself and the world. His entire attitude about life in general was different. Fritz remembered Uncle Sunday reading to him that if a man is in Christ, he is a new person.

"I'm going to return home a different way from my trip west," Fritz reasoned. "I want no more of the Ocoee River, and I want to visit my Cherokee friends. This may be my final opportunity. Once I get Willa, I'll never see these mountains again. I'm going to purchase all the supplies I can haul and take them to the Indians. In my opinion, our government has given them a raw deal."

"Now that's another thing I admire about you. You're always thinking about others. You amaze me, my boy. And another thing, Fritz, I had a talk with God last night. I believe I made peace with him."

In Murphy, just like Ike predicted, Fritz and Franz chose the road less taken into the heart of the Great Smoky Mountains and across Soco Gap.

Lyndon had loosed the strap that held his new Springfield .50 caliber and loaded a cartridge into the chamber. There was little doubt he planned to shoot the Pinkerton in the back and retrieve his money.

It was as if Ike read the crook's mind. Before he rode away, he gave a chilling gaze and held it until fear shook the nerve of Lyndon. He stepped his horse sideways, watching him, until he was out of sight.

Now it was only Lyndon, the gambler and the murderer, on the trail of men who were pursuing new dreams and fresh beginnings. He stayed far behind, lest he be seen by those he pursued. His plans were to, in some way, pass them and get far enough ahead to lay an ambush and shoot from above them. He followed for two more days until they stopped over in Andrews.

They rented a room and ate well before Fritz went to the mercantile trading post and bought as much as he could haul to his Indian friends—salt, traps, knives, axes, bright cloth for the women, needles, thread, buttons, and tea. He bought used but good rifles the armies had used and much ammunition for the weapons. These he knew were needed for hunting game food. He knew the Cherokees were not notorious man killers. He also bought tobacco—most precious to the Indians. He was like a child, waiting to see his friends and present their gifts.

It was in Andrews that Lyndon made his move. During the night, he moved around and ahead of them.

From Andrews, the road was terrible. At times Fritz feared the carriage might not negotiate it, especially around rock bluffs projecting out over the mountain road. The road dodged through coves and around hills, doubling on itself, and then crept up grades at the only possible angle. He dreaded the most terrifying place of all—the gorge through which the Nantahala River tumbled, whitewater almost the entire stretch.

Lord, don't let another flood come like the one I went through in the Ocoee River gorge. That was one experience I will never forget. They managed to pass through with only one or two frightening experiences.

On a ridge top, Fritz put up a smoke signal and waited. Before dark, an Indian came who did not know him, soon another, then another, all from different directions. Finally, Buck Standingdeer's brother, Andy, appeared, and the whoops began. He led them to a small, secluded village of about four dozen Cherokees, and as did Buck, Andy could communicate a little in English.

"This is Sky Boys," Andy told the tribe. "Son of family that helped us since we fled back to our Smoky Mountain home. We must welcome him, our guest."

As if hurry was not in the Indian vocabulary, the time of jubilation was long and happy. Franz, awed by all the merriment around him, was finally introduced as a friend of Sky Boys. Sky's heart leaped to hear his real name again. He felt safe here, if nowhere else.

Then came the opening of gifts—necessities all needed for the Indian's meager existence. They were overjoyed.

Sky, dreading the duty, explained the circumstance and death of his friends and guides, Buck Standingdeer and Goliath Chicalili. Having heard nothing, the tribe was not surprised at the report.

The tribe insisted Sky and Franz spend the night. The sights, scents, and poverty were beyond Franz's comprehension.

At sunrise, the two men were on their way. Deep in the forest, Sky pulled off the road and suggested to Franz, "I have a feeling we should take the time to check our gold under the false floor." They loosened the screws, lifted the top lid, and there it was, all secure on the bottom floor: the thousands of dollars in shimmering gold coins. They spread the cover back into place and moved along. Up, up, and higher still they meandered along the road, which followed the old buffalo and elk trails. It was touch and go all the way. At times, Sky had to dig and shovel the road wider for the carriage to proceed. Below were hundreds of feet, a sheer mountain with scrub trees clinging to crevasses in boulders that had been washed over with waters of Soco Creek in eons past. Sky shuddered at the frightful sight.

Above them a large flat boulder hung out over the trail. Growing over it were a few scattered bushes.

Lying in wait, on his belly, was Lyndon James whose diabolical hatred had driven him to murder. The bead of his .50 caliber Springfield was on the chest of Franz. He touched the trigger, and Franz never knew what hit him. It was a heart shot, dead center.

Sky on instinct grabbed his Henry and jumped off the seat on the inside of the road. A second boom from the giant gun hit the rib cage of one of the harnessed horses. It fell off the road, pulling the other two horses and the carriage off into the canyon below.

Everything was deathly quiet. Sky had no idea who had shot Franz. He waited without moving under the cover of a thick mountain laurel bush. In a moment, a pebble fell from above. Something or someone had stirred. Another stone rolled. He remained rigid, waiting. At long last, a figure moved into the road ahead. *So he's the one, Lyndon James, the man who tried to drown Franz in the Mississippi waters and who had, without doubt, hired the two black legs to kidnap and kill Franz the second time. This third attempt was fatal.*

He was ambivalent. He had never planned to kill anyone. Even Rosco had left him no choice. It registered in Sky's mind that the man was lifting his gun straight at him.

He was no rifleman. He had shot very few guns, but by instinct, he lifted his Henry rifle and pulled the trigger. Lyndon staggered, seeking balance. He moved his Springfield slightly, and Sky levered the Henry and blasted another .44 slug into him. He fell and plunged over the cliff.

Sky became suddenly sick and lost the contents of his stomach. He sat breathing hard, trying in some way to put reality back together about what had transpired.

I'm alone in strange country. Everything I own for the trip is hopelessly lost, lying hundreds of feet out of reach.

Then he remembered. *I have friends, the Indians, and I can trust them.* He headed back down the trail beside Soco Creek, and within two hours, he walked into their camp.

The Indians read trouble in his body language. Andy approached him with concern.

"No wheels? No friend?"

"An enemy of my friend waylaid us. He shot my friend, and our outfit went off the cliff under the flat rock that hangs over the road just this side of Soco Gap. It is impossible to retrieve it."

"Unh, other bad white man. Indians say cuss words for them."

He explained his dilemma and his intention to get his sweetheart. "I am in strange country here. Would you guide me to the old Cherokee site where the Swannanoa meets the French Broad River? That's the village site of your grandfathers."

"Sky Boys need no ask. You brother. Boys family save my family back many moons. I help, glad."

The name Sky had a ring to it. Its sound was like the strum of a finely tuned instrument and deeply touched his heart.

Sky and Andy locked hands on each other's wrist and touched their hearts with the other. Sky smiled. Andy was stoic. Both meant the same thing.

Next morning, Andy, with his shoulder bag and bow with arrows, walked ahead of Sky into the heart of the Great Smoky Mountains. Sky's possessions were his clothes, a few coins in his pocket, a knife, his Henry rifle, and thirteen cartridges.

"Sky rest, this night. Eat. We leave, sunrise."

When Sky and Andy reached the flat rock overhang, they looked over. Down hundreds of feet, suspended on another rock projection, hung the carriage, badly torn apart. The horses were out of sight. Lyndon was dangling upside down, hanging in the fork of a tree.

"Unh. Good buzzard meat." Andy said no more.

"Mark this spot, friend." Sky pointed. "In between the two floors of that carriage are thousands of dollars in gold money, wampum." By the quizzical look on Andy's face, he knew he had not communicated. He tried again.

"In wagon…bottom." Sky put his hands together, one on top the other, and squatted as if sitting. "Down yonder." Sky pulled his few remaining gold coins from his pocket. "Many, many of these." Andy only looked at him. "They are yours, Andy, if you can get them."

"Hell no. Indian life more than gold. No need." Andy turned and proceeded up the road toward Soco Gap.

Andy struck a fire to break the high altitude night chill. The two friends shared a morsel of jerky in the gap at Soco, more than a mile above sea level.

"Home." Andy touched Sky. "Far, toward sunup." He pointed east. "Many suns." He waved his hand in an arch from east to west and flashed ten fingers two times.

Twenty more days, Sky counted.

"Indian stay off white man road. Sky stay off or…" Andy put his hands around his neck and jerked upward, his tongue hanging out. Andy chuckled like that was funny. Sky didn't think so.

Sky was walking on the ground, his shoe soles worn through, leaving large holes. That evening at dusk Andy killed a deer and trimmed its hide to wrap around his shoes, secured with strips cut from the hide.

"Eat good, Sky, me. Next sun, go far."

They made a wide circle to the north around Waynesville. In the small village of Canton, Sky left Andy and went to the trading post to buy a pair of shoes. He felt somewhat safe with his long beard and hair and with a band around his head, Indian style.

He was paralyzed with fear when he saw the wanted poster, dead or alive.

Wearing new shoes, Sky brought back to Andy a new sheath knife and a do-pretty for his squaw.

"Andy, you must turn back. I can find my way home from here. One or two more days and I'll be there."

"Andy go. I said—"

"No. I have bad news. A reward is posted for me dead or alive. I must go alone. You must turn back. I thank you."

"No thank Andy. Sky family, brother."

"I'll not need this rifle anymore. From here on, it could only lead me into more trouble. Take it. My gift to you. There are…" Sky pondered, *How do I say this?* He held up his ten fingers and then three more. Andy smiled. "There is more ammunition to use in this rifle among the things I brought to the tribe."

He watched with sadness as Andy blended into the forest.

CHAPTER 13

Willa, at times, felt her separation from Sky unbearable. The emotional wounds that had been opened by the condemnation of the love of her life were bleeding her to death. She longed to rekindle the old fire from the embers of their friendship and love. She could only exist. Day by day she survived on the single crust of the moment she and Sky pledged themselves to each other. It was then her world began. It ended when he was torn away from her and condemned by a group of vigilantes whose only motive was hatred and retaliation for a lost cause.

Was he alive or dead? She knew in her heart of hearts if he was alive, he would someday, some night, some way come for her, and she was prepared, waiting for that moment. Nothing or no one could hold her back if and when he came.

Her friends, many of them, were not helpful. "What if he is dead?" "If he does return, he will be caught?" Others said, "Why waste your life and years?" Her reply was unshakeable. "I've listened to the voice of my heart. I'm waiting for Sky. I feel he is alive. I feel him connected to me. That is the voice of my soul."

The parents of Willa Goodson meant well. They too loved Sky, but reality faced them also. At their insistence, she allowed herself to be escorted by gentlemen to religious meetings and social gatherings. Beautiful and socially groomed, she was a prize to be won, but her heart was fixed, and she kept herself for her one and only, Sky Boys.

After much persuasion, she agreed to go to college. "An education can be an asset for any woman," her father tactfully advised her. "I will support you in any field you choose to pursue. You would make a good teacher," he suggested.

"Oh no, Father. If I go to college, I'll study law and become a lawyer and go after the crooks in the legal system like those who robbed me of my darling Sky." Willa's jaw was set. "However, with respect to you and Mother, if Sky returns for me, I will be with him to my dying day."

She moved away from home and family to begin college in pursuit of a law degree.

Her first research assignment was how to search out accused criminals who have never been apprehended. She requested her first research paper be narrowed to western North Carolina, and her petition was granted.

Her stratagem was to learn the origin, the operation, and history of a man known only as Brisco. It was like searching for a wart on an elephant. No one knew anything except a few who had only heard of Brisco, and none of them could give her any substantial evidence.

One day a gift fell as if from heaven, a wanted bulletin, long filed away in a sheriff's desk drawer: "Wanted.

Information about a man or two men who rob and kill travelers, always in remote places. Last victim, Clarence Nevels."

Willa immediately rented a horse and made a beeline to Asheville, passing the bulletin to the lawyer of Sky and Sunday. Anthony Chandler was in his carriage within an hour heading to the source of the information.

Willa returned to school for her final examinations. She was eager to come back home in two more days.

It appeared at first to lead to a dead end, but good attorneys need only a vague sniff. "Give me the names, Sheriff, of any you know who were killed or robbed by this person or persons."

"I only know of the one who was killed in my county, a wealthy man whose business required travel. He was robbed and killed, leaving no trace that I could find."

"Give every particular you can about this victim, even minute details."

"Well, his name was Clarence Nevels, maybe in his forties, wore good clothes, you know, clothes that you would wear to church."

"Did he wear a ring, a tie pin, a watch? Did he carry a weapon?"

"As a matter of fact, he did. A fancy gold watch, and I would suspect he carried a pistol. Most folks do, you know. Even though we've about stopped the Bushwhackers, a few of them still fool around."

"Could this have been, in your opinion, a Bushwhacker?"

"Naw, I don't think so. I saw no evidence of that."

"Did you say he carried money?"

"Yes, his widow told me he left home with ten twenty-dollar gold coins in a pouch and some bills. Change maybe."

"Did he travel in a buggy or ride a horse?"

"Now there's one I haven't figured out yet. The widow told me his horse never showed up, a fine Arabian, but somebody brought in a stray horse a couple of days later, and nobody claimed it. Beats me."

"Sheriff, you've been a considerable help. I know the people in your county are proud to have a man like you."

"Why, thank you, sir. That's always good to hear."

As the lawyer pulled away, the sheriff ran out and hailed him. "Just between us, Clarence was a little peaked, and he usually stashed away a jug. You know, for his belly ache and such."

"Of course, and thank you. All of us need some medicine all along."

Anthony Chandler was enlivened, like a Plott hound on a bear trail.

Now he needed a court order, but the shrewd lawyer knew he had to work completely without the knowledge or suspicion of Sheriff Zack Pearson, whom he had suspected had set up the abuse of justice for Sky's troubles from the beginning.

Sunday's incarceration was justified, but it was Zack, he suspected all along, who set the entire matter in motion for his arrest.

The court order to examine the evidence used in the Sky Boys murder trial was obtained out of Raleigh, through telegraph issued from another county.

Anthony waited until he knew Zack was out of the county, and he hit the Buncombe County court records for the evidence he sought.

There they were, diamonds, in a pile of coal: the watch Sky had turned in to the sheriff as having been won from the man, Brisco, in a poker game with the name "Clarence Nevels" engraved on the case, the pouch containing ten twenty-dollar gold coins, and a fancy custom-made saddle with the name carved in the leather behind the cantle, "C. Nevels."

A veritable gold mine, the mother lode.

Tony told no one anything, not even his client in jail. This was the crown jewel case of his life. He did not dare to leave one legal stone unturned.

The lawyer hated the hair-raising road down the mountain to Old Fort. He wondered how on earth they would ever get a railroad up the mountain with straight up and down ridges of solid granite. No wonder every town had railroads except Asheville. *Maybe someday*, he mused. He had other matters on his mind now.

Without asking questions from the sheriff, Anthony Chandler checked records, dates, names, witnesses... and then, glory be to the Almighty! A man had been found dead by a prospector, June 15, 1870. Items found on body: an 1849 Colt pistol with "C. Nevels" carved on the butt of its wooden grip. There was an ivory-handled knife, scrimshawed on one handle a whaling scene, and on the other, *To Brisco from Rosco. Congratulations.*

Congratulations indeed! One happy lawyer went back up the Black Mountains, which he found nowhere near the steep grade as before. His poor horse could not carry him up rapidly enough.

The next person on Tony's agenda was the man who swore he saw the fight when Sky was accused of killing Brisco. After a lengthy search, he found a man who said he knew that witness. "He got religion at the Methodist Camp Meeting."

The dates, Tony pondered. "That camp meeting was conducted on what dates?"

"Gosh, I donno," the man said. "I ain't got no calendar. Couldn't read it if'n I had one, but it's always the first day of June and goes two weeks or longer." The man lowered his voice as if to confide in the lawyer. "I got religion too, I did."

"Good, good. Do you remember which nights this man who professed religion attended the meeting?'

"Why, shore I do. He come ever night. Truth is, he sat beside me and talked me into going to the altar with him. That's a fact."

"Sir, you are a good man. You continue following God. It will do you good now and in the life to come."

"Hallelujah, praise God!" the man shouted as he walked away.

Before dark and while he had a head of steam, Tony knocked on the door of the former bootlegger, who was a sworn witness at Sky Boys's trial.

"I need some information from you, sir, about your testimony on the stand, under oath. I'm concerned about what you saw on the night you said you saw Sky Boys hit a man over the head and kill him."

"Now, feller, I don't wanna talk 'bout that thar trial, nairy other time. Hit's over and done."

"No, it isn't. Now I know you made peace with God at that meeting. That's good. I'm happy for you. But I must advise you, if you didn't tell the whole truth about what you said you saw, you could be in very serious trouble. Fact is, you could go to jail a long time. The law calls it perjury." Tony let that soak in. The lawyer stretched the truth a bit. "I know a lot of people who saw you at that camp meeting. They say you were there in attendance every single night."

The man was visibly shaken, his face livid.

"Mister lawyer, sir, I was wrong. I lied. I did. Sheriff Pearson paid me five dollars. I didn't have no job. I jest flat-out lied. That's what I done."

"Thank you for your honesty, sir. This testimony you've given me now could be the end of your involvement. But if it isn't, I promise to plea the court to go light on you."

"I'm much obliged to you, sir. Thank ye."

Oh, my lord, Anthony Chandler mused. *How many people can this involve? Sheriff Pearson, Judge Alex Cogdil and his assistant William Rodgers, the poor sheriff Creed Gamble, and heaven only knows who else.*

In spite of the fact Sunday Boys was in Zack Pearson's filthy jail and wanting to get out, Tony knew not to tilt his hand. Every jot and tittle had to be substantiated and in order.

When his case was complete, he telegraphed Raleigh, giving his findings and requested a state court official be dispatched to arrest Sheriff Zackary Pearson and to supervise the case, one that could set a precedent for the entire western North Carolina system of justice.

The official arrived by train in Salisbury four days later. Tony had assigned a driver to pick him up and bring him by carriage to Asheville.

The hammer fell and hit like a sledge on an anvil.

Sunday Boys was immediately released from jail. Because of his education and limited legal knowledge, the court appointed him to serve as temporary sheriff until the upcoming election.

Sherrif Zackary Pearson, however, was nowhere to be found.

Sky Boys was exonerated of all charges, but everyone had questions. Where was Sky? Was he somewhere in Texas? Uncle Sunday had pointed him in that direction. Was he alive? How could they ever find him? Must he always be under a cloud of fear and suspicion, never knowing his name had been cleared? What if someone saw the dead or alive poster and killed the innocent man? And just as important, where was the sheriff, the man who instigated everything in the first place?

Willa knew the love of her life was a free man, but did he know that he was now liberated from the death sentence? Would she ever see him again? Must she live to the end of her life alone and lonely?

CHAPTER 14

“Sheriff Boys, I’m afeared thar’s trouble abrewing over in Haywood. That family of Brackins boys hear’d that somebody had seed Sky Boys at the trad’n post in Canton th’ other day.” The mountain man spat his tobacco juice and wiped his chin. “That was ’fore you’uns took down them word signs awant’n’ him. They’s all bunched up to go git him and claim the reward money. Ever one of um’s tot’n a pistol and rifle gun. I ‘eard that they’d gotten the sheriff wit’ ‘em. I know’d ye’d want to hear ’bout it.”

“I do, Elmer. Thank you very much. It’s good people like you are making our mountains a better place.”

Sunday turned to his deputy. “Gather up six or eight good men as quickly as possible. I’ll deputize them and try to call these men off. They’re a mean bunch of crooks and scalawags to start with. Trigger-happy game poachers every one of them.”

The informant seemed amazed at the efficiency of the new sheriff. “Elmer, did you hear where those Brackins boys are searching for Sky?”

“The way it come to me wus they b’lieved he wus treed up in the Newfound Mount’n, summers up thar. That’s wild country, it is.”

"Did you hear why they thought it was Sky they saw?"

"Wa'll they said he was a redhead, sorta strawberry-like an' had a beard and long hair. That liddle quicky-step they said give 'im away." Elmer cleared his mouth again, wiping the corner creases this time. "He was foller'n foot and game trails, stay'n off the main road. That's 'bout all I kin tell ye, Sheriff. I hope it heps ye."

In less than an hour, Sunday had his posse organized. He gave them quick instructions, and they struck out on horseback. They forded the French Broad, turned up Hominy Creek, and followed it until it was only a branch. Holland Mountain towered above them on the north.

"It won't be long before dark. You men rest up tonight. I'll push on to Canton in the moonlight and try to gather something solid we can go on tomorrow."

Sunday rode to Canton, hitched his horse at the trading post, and slept until the owner came in to open up.

"Yes, Sheriff Boys, that young feller you're asking about was here. He bought a pair of shoes." He fetched Sky's abandoned pair with deerskin laced around them to protect his feet from the ground. The trader shook his head. "He looked a sight, Sheriff, like he'd come a far piece." He pulled a five-dollar gold coin from his pocket. "He paid me with this. I had to run up to the house to get change. That's the first gold coin I've ever seen. He took his change and left. He was a man of few words."

"Tell me everything you remember."

"Well, he was about my size in height. Fatten him up some, he'd be bigger. He was redheaded, pretty near the color of that clay bank over there. His hair was long, and he had a beard. He had this kind of quick step, sorta like he walked from his knees down, but he was moving along fast when he left."

The trader studied. "Oh yeah, there was a feller here from over your way, in Buncombe. He studied your man pretty hard. In fact, I think his eyeing him made your feller spooky. When your man left, he went down yonder. You see that big poplar tree? He turned up the main trail that goes up Holland Mountain."

"Tell me about the man you say was from Buncombe."

"He said to me, 'That there was Sky Boys, the escaped murderer.' I told him I heard Sky Boys had been freed somehow by the court, that they found out he was innocent. Anyway, he tore out east atrottin' his horse. Didn't buy a blessed thing. Nothing."

"Listen to me, sir. It is important to me. That man, Sky Boys, has been acquitted. He has been declared innocent by the court. The reward offered for him has been lifted. I need to find him before someone tries to kill him for the reward money—there is no reward anymore. Sky Boys is a free man."

Sunday had an itch. He kept scratching at the trader believing he was holding something back from him.

"Well, Sheriff, a man in my business has to be careful, you know, mind his own business." He looked left and right then made one step closer to Sunday and said, "Since you told me like it is, I'll tell you this. Nine rough-looking fellers rode in here two days ago. One of 'em was that sheriff, Zackary Pearsons. They said the Boys feller was seen here and asked me which way he went. I told them up yonder way, the trail to Billie Top. They lit out up in that direction."

"And as far as you know, they haven't come back down?"

"Not while I've been here."

"You have helped me. Thank you. I'll try to send some business your way."

Sunday rode back to his group of worried men. "We were fixin' to come huntin' you."

Sunday gave them the report. "Do any of you have knowledge about Holland Mountain?"

"Oh yes," one spoke, "I've hunted bear all over it. There are six main trails that go all the way over to Newfound on the other side."

Sunday sent one man up each trail, instructing them if they found any kind of solid information to shoot three times and they'd all merge to him. The six spread out. Two remained with Sunday, hoping, praying the bounty hunters did not find Sky traveling on foot before they did.

The search was on. Sky's life was again at stake.

Two days later, Sunday signaled the posse together. "We've combed the woods, studied every trail. None of us has found a speck of evidence that Sky was there. As badly as I hate to, we'll call it off and go home. My only hope is that the Brackins boys don't find and kill him. When he left the trading post, he vanished. Buck Standingdeer must have taught him well."

The past year had matured Sky into a wily fox, plenty gun-shy and knowing the evil in some men's hearts.

He suspected the man at the trading post had recognized him by his actions and intentionally headed north toward Holland Mountain in the Newfound Range, a wild and tangled place.

Sky waited until dark and crossed the road, careful to leave no sign, and headed due south, setting his aim to the mile-high Mount Pisgah. It was a fierce climb, but his life was at stake. That fact he knew, and he pressed on. He wasn't certain, but he figured he had outmaneuvered them. He stayed in dense brush and thickets where no horse could travel. Buck Standingdeer and Andy had taught him mountain skills that few white men knew.

After topping Pisgah to the south, he turned back northeasterly following the ridgeline to the Shut-in Trail to the French Broad and waded the river at Sandy Bottom to the eastern shore.

From there, his excitement built. Ten more miles. Best.

His plans had all been disrupted. He looked like a tramp, his clothes in shreds, hair disheveled, and only God knew the looks of his shaggy beard.

What will Willa say when she sees me? Will she even recognize me? Tired and weary, he even asked himself, *What if she won't leave with me? I only have a few dollars left. How will I care for her? Where will we go—and how?*

The joys of his yesterdays turned to doubt and fear today. He pressed on now, rounding the big horseshoe bend of the French Broad.

When he entered Best, it was past midnight traveling by the light of a full moon. First he tapped on the door of Uncle Sunday, twice, three times. No answer. Dejected and confused, he went to the Goodson house, the home of Willa.

He put his knuckle to the front door. He waited. A stir. A lamplight. A crack in the door. Lamplight fell on his face.

"It's Sky!" Mr. Goodson yelled. "It's Sky! He's come home!"

Willa ran down the stairway three steps at a time. She ran into his arms, weeping for joy. "Oh my darling, my love, you're home!"

Sky embraced her as if his life depended on it, and indeed it did. His entire journey had only had one guiding light: Willa. He cried tears of joy as he held her. He was finally home.

Sky wiped the tears from his eyes and looked at Willa. "My love, we have to leave. It's not safe here."

"Leave?" she cried. "We don't have to leave. You are a free man. Exonerated. Free!"

In the distance, a galloping horse whinnied, and a voice boomed, "Is that Sky Boys? The murderer who faked his death?"

Sky's heart stopped. He turned around and saw nine rough-looking men on horseback, armed to the teeth. Zackary Pearson trotted his horse up to Sky and Willa.

"I gotta admit to ya, kid, you almost had me. I really thought you had died that day. I'll tell you one thing though: ya never should have come back."

The ex-sheriff hopped off his horse, revolver in hand, and marched up to Sky. The smell of alcohol permeated the air. He put the barrel of his gun on Sky's forehead.

"It's clear that we can't trust our fine judicial system to bring justice to this murderer. So"—he pulled back the hammer on his revolver—"I'll just do it myself."

Sky shut his eyes and braced himself for the end.

The shot rang out through the air, but the end never came.

Zackary Pearson looked perplexed and then fell to the ground, dead. Behind him stood Sunday Boys, rifle in hand, flanked by his posse. Sky's heart leapt.

"Uncle Sunday!"

"Sky Boys! I have to admit, I wasn't sure this day would ever come, but I thank God Almighty that it has."

Sunday got off his horse and embraced Sky. Once again, tears of joy fell from Sky's eyes. His troubles were finally over.

He turned to Willa. "Everything is finally back to normal. Willa, I love you so much. There wasn't a day that went by that I wasn't thinking about you. All I want to do is just be with you every second of every day, to start a family with you—"

Willa's mother stepped from behind Willa and handed her a little girl with red curls. Willa smiled.

"We already have a family, Sky. Her name is Sunshine. Remember that day before our lives fell apart? The time we spent under the willow tree?"

Sky smiled. "This is our daughter."

Life settled down for Sky, Sunday, and Willa. Sunday went on to become the greatest sheriff the county had ever seen, and Sky, Willa, and Sunshine lived out the rest of their days in happiness. Every once in a while, though, Sky would look back upon the adventures he had on his Smoky Mountain odyssey. And every time he would think about it, he would say, "I've finally made it home."

Afterword

From this book's inception, every idea, every page was inspired by God Almighty. His Holy Spirit guided its development and choice of publisher, all to the praise of Jesus Christ.

Bill Penley was bred, born, and reared in the foothills of the Great Smoky Mountains. He roamed, fished, and hunted under her shadows his entire life. Except for nine years he spent in college and graduate school, he has never lived beyond a hoot and hollow from the place of his birth.

Bill Penley's two previous books and numerous magazine articles were written under the pen name "The Mountain Man," a name he has carried throughout his professional life.

Prior to embarking on a career of writing, Bill Penley made his living as a public speaker storyteller. Audiences sat in amazement as his words were transformed into a thousand pictures from his mental library of mountain lore, legends, myths, and anecdotes.

Bill Penley has spoken on every continent except Australia, inspiring lives even when his words were delivered via an interpreter. He once said, "The inner needs of people worldwide are basically the same, be they in the heart of Russia, the boardrooms of America, or in the shops and offices of every city. Humankind yearns to be accepted, loved, and challenged."

A severe accident made it impossible to continue the ruthless demands of travel; thus, he now writes to show his life experiences and knowledge.

Promo

In your hands is a historical novel set in the ruins of post-Civil War western North Carolina. You will revisit a region raped and ravaged by both Confederate and Union troops. The protagonist, Sky Boys, is a young man who escaped the war's carnage but was convicted of murder and sentenced to hang. His miraculous getaway, his life on the lam, and longing for his betrothed, Willa, will turn a few minutes of reading time into hours.

This fictional novel is geographically and historically correct. In it you will discover nuggets about the Appalachian heritage flowing like rivulets into mountain streams. You will recognize integrity and deceit, daring and cowardice, hatred and love, all woven into a masterful, dramatic conflict.

Foremost, readers will perceive how Sky's Christian faith guarded him in times of danger and death.